SHUT THE DOOR

SHUT THE DOOR

MAUREEN FLYNN

PEMMICAN
PUBLICATIONS
INC.

Pemmican Publications gratefully acknowledges the assistance accorded to its publishing program by Canada Council for the Arts, Canadian Heritage – Canada Book Fund, the Manitoba Arts Council, and the Province of Manitoba through the Book Publishing Tax Credit and the Book Publisher Marketing Assistance Program.

Design & Typography by Relish New Brand Experience

Printed and Bound in Canada.

First printing: 2015

LIBRARY AND ARCHIVES CANADA CATALOGUING IN PUBLICATION

Flynn, Maureen, 1960-, author

    Shut the door / Maureen Flynn.

ISBN 978-1-894717-97-7 (paperback)

    I. Title.

PS8611.L95S58 2015   C813'.6   C2015-905014-6

PEMMICAN PUBLICATIONS INC.

Committed to the promotion of Metis culture and heritage

150 Henry Avenue, Winnipeg, Manitoba
R3B 0J7 Canada
www.pemmicanpublications.ca

for
Hudson
Bridget, Mike and Mark
And in loving memory of Don Flynn

PROLOGUE

Friday, February 14, 1947

"It was the snow!"

Nadine's scream was maniacal, barely recognizable as human. She banged on the window with one hand, then the other, over and over again. Her clenched fists hit the panes harder and faster as tears streamed down her face. She barely noticed when the glass shattered, and only continued her efforts with increased strength, pounding now at nothing but a gaping hole. Blood spurted out of the gashes she had suffered from the broken shards. Rich crimson droplets fell on the snowy white sill. She felt no pain.

Defeated, she dropped her arms to rest, and minded the blood oozing from her wounds. Her tears had ceased, and she stood frozen, staring blankly beyond the window, toward the darkness.

When a blast of cold wind gusted through the broken window, it roused her from the trance-like spirit that had overcome her, and returned a slight sense of awareness. Enough to make her remember. As the icy air swept through her, past her, she rose. A deathly chill gripped the once-warm room. Gusts continued to blow, and soon swirls of snow followed.

Nadine went mad. She ran around the room, chasing the snow-flakes, cursing their very existence. To her dismay, they were fleeting, gone before she could derive the satisfaction of finishing them herself. Many blew and landed on the wall. Nadine pressed her body against that wall and slammed her bare hands against it in utter despair. Once again, tears fell from her eyes and ran down her face. Her blood splattered on the rose-petal wallpaper and trickled lazily down the wall.

Squeezing her eyes shut, she prayed for it all to go away.

CHAPTER ONE

Sunday, November 17, 2013

"Helllp meeee!"

Steve Ascot woke with a start. As disoriented as he was, he managed to leap to his feet. His right hand went instinctively to where his gun holster would hang. He stood ready. He scanned the room with squinted eyes. A sound to his right alerted him; he spun in that direction.

What was it? Who was it? Then he heard it again—it was a laugh. He instantly realized where he was…and the laugh? It was Penny. There was obviously no imminent danger, to himself, or anyone else. He was in his own living room. The TV blared loudly. A horror movie played on the screen.

Penny sat at the table, still grinning. "You OK, Steve? You fell asleep on the couch."

A sheepish smile formed on Steve's face as he realized his subconscious had merely been duped by the phony screams from a creepy flick. Feeling foolish, he grabbed the remote and switched the TV off.

Penny had already resumed her fast-paced clicking on the keyboard. Steve stood and watched her a moment. He was a tall man, just shy of 6-2. Normally his stature alone commanded at least some attention, but when Penny was writing, he may as well be invisible. He regretted that she had even noticed him leap from the couch in the first place.

Stretching his arms high in the air, he released a loud yawn and then dropped his arms and clasped his hands behind his head. His eyes stung; he was tired. May as well go to bed, he thought. Once she was on a roll, who knew how long she'd be up? As he headed toward the bedroom, he paused when he heard the clicking halt. He turned back to look in her direction.

Penny peered over her new reading glasses. "Going to bed?"

"May as well."

"I'll probably stay tonight, 'k?"

"Sure. Just turn the lights out when you're done."

He had barely got the words out when the clicking resumed.

Steve flicked on the bedroom light. He reached in the closet for his housecoat, a red tartan flannel—his favourite. He had always prized it for the comfort; the fact that it looked mighty decent on him was a bonus. For some reason, Penny thought it looked ridiculous.

He remembered the first time he put it on in front of her. They had been enjoying an especially romantic evening together and as he stood slowly tying the belt, he was pleased to notice her looking up at him from the bed. Yes he was smug, or was before he noticed Penny's chest beginning to rise and fall in short, fast heaves; even the bed shook. And there it was. She covered her mouth with both hands just before her burst of laughter filled the room. "What? What?" he had asked, and then demanded. All she could do was point at him and blurt out, "Housecoat!" Her laugh continued as she pounded her fist on the bed. Tears of laughter followed.

Steve was insulted, but her laughter was contagious. He even provoked it by strutting around the room in regal fashion. Later she apologized and he admitted, in fake seriousness, how hurt he had been by her reaction. After that, whenever she made fun of his housecoat he would bluff hurt and insulted, and enjoy the fact that she would have to hold her tongue and perhaps keep a lid on her laughter.

Steve stepped into the shower. He closed his eyes while the warm water poured over his face. Rubbing both hands through his thick dark hair, he pushed it back from his face. The relaxing solitude allowed his mind to wander. He felt good. Tomorrow he would be back, officially, at his real job, homicide detective for the Winnipeg police. He could scarcely believe now that he had ever left, but at the time, it was his only choice.

The reality was he had shot and killed a murder suspect. The man's name was forever ingrained in Steve's head—Jim Kobac. Steve had hated him, or at least his kind. The man had no humanity, treated woman like dirt. He saw them only as a means for lining his own pocket, and if circumstances dictated, these women were dispensable. Still, Steve was remorseful. Kobac was still a human being, and he had taken the man's life. If all had gone right he would have got a conviction, locked Kobac up for a long time, but that's not what happened.

Everyone else had accepted the fact that Steve had shot him in self-defence—everyone but Steve. With the sole witness recanting, Steve knew it was unlikely they'd pin the murder on Kobac, and he'd walk. Was that the real reason he had pulled the trigger or was it truly to protect himself? Steve just didn't know. It was this uncertainty that had drove him to finally walk away from the force. Leave the job he loved. Leave the life that defined his very soul.

Shortly after he left, Steve's life took a downward spiral. The torment of his uncertainty and the fact that he didn't even know who he was anymore, all contributed to his downfall. It didn't last forever, though. Being the man he is, Steve forced himself to crawl out of his mess. Eventually he found himself a new job, head of hotel security at the Marlborough Hotel. That is when things really began to turn around for him. A series of staggering events at the hotel had made it obvious to Steve how important it was for him to be back on the force. He belonged there, they needed him, and more than anything, he longed to be back on the job. Now he could. The hotel events had him finally come to the realization that Jim Kobac was killed truly in self-defence. Steve could go back to his work.

Regardless, self-defence or not, Steve continued to regret the outcome. He did take some solace in knowing that Kobac would never have the chance to murder again. Steve strongly believed that a murderer should never be given the chance to kill again. It's what made his work so important. You can't always prevent a murder, but when one happens, and if you're good, you can find out who did it. If you conduct a thorough investigation and gather the right evidence, and can prove it, you just might put them away for a long time.

As pleased as he was to be going back, Steve didn't regret any of his time working at the Marlborough. I t was also where he had met Penny. It was she who had helped him realize many truths, made him believe in himself again. She also had him believing in other things, things you couldn't always see with your eyes, but could sense. He wouldn't admit this to her, but he couldn't totally deny it anymore either, and sometimes, he found himself—

"Boo!"

Steve jerked and swung the shower curtain open. "What the—"

It was Penny.

"You should never startle a person in my line of work, Penny." He stood taller to gain some authority, but in his present state he failed miserably.

She was sitting on the fuzzy toilet seat, hunched over, pretending to cover her eyes but peeking through the slits of her fingers.

Steve put his hands on his hips and smiled at her. Penny smiled back.

"You better either get in here now...or get out quick!"

Penny laughed and scrambled out in a hurry.

Peaking out of the curtain he watched her exit, a trail of red tartan behind her. She had taken his housecoat! He rolled his eyes, cut his shower short and chased after her.

CHAPTER TWO

The alarm clock on Steve's bedside table buzzed loudly. He flung his arm in the direction of the sound and fumbled until he found the snooze button. He glanced over at Penny. It was too early for her to wake up. One look and he realized he needn't have worried; she was dead to the world. The alarm had had no effect on her. He decided to lie there for just a few more minutes, promising himself just long enough to collect his thoughts. The bedroom curtains were wide open, yet the room remained dark. The days were short this time of year and the sun wouldn't be up for another hour or so.

The dream he had been having was still with him, in bits. He tried to remember more. He closed his eyes and concentrated. It had been snowing, and he was outside on a road. What was he holding? A hockey stick—and he realized he was still just a kid. He was playing street hockey with his brother and some kids from the old neighbourhood. He looked down. The puck was on his stick. Some of the kids were yelling. "Go! Go, Steve!" He ran with the puck, but just as he was about to shoot, the buzzer sounded.

A buzzer in street hockey—he jolted awake, realizing the buzzer was his alarm going off again. "Oh crap!" He had fallen back to sleep. He jumped out of bed and reached to shut the alarm off. As he did, he realized he had better get moving. Today was his first day with his partner, his first partner since his return to work. It had been a lengthy leave. The last few months were spent mostly reintegrating back into the department, on paperwork and getting up to speed on new safety regulations. Plus, of course, the current case load. He was really pumped to get back out on the streets, even if he had to break in a new partner, and he sure didn't want to be late.

He got ready quickly, and before he knew it he was riding the apartment elevator down to the underground parking. Steve loved the indoor parking. The parkade was a dingy place, but at least he didn't have to go outside and start a cold car. The November warm spell they had been enjoying had ended abruptly. It was now running around -30, and they already had their fair share of the white stuff. Steve didn't mind winter, but he hated scraping windows and brushing snow off the car. He'd done it long enough and considered it a waste of his time, especially on mornings like today.

The radio blared when he turned on the ignition, and he smiled. Penny must have driven it last. He turned down the radio, snapped on his belt, and expertly manoeuvred the sharp parkade curves until he reached the exit that sent him out to the dark city streets. It was early; the city was silent. Somehow, fresh fallen snow always had a way of making the streets quieter.

Turning the radio up again, he switched to the classic rock station and remembered when it was just called rock. He still missed Tom and Joe, the morning DJs, whose banter he had listened to since he was a teenager. A song by Streetheart was playing, one of his favourite local bands. He turned the volume up and sang along, as he sometimes did, but only when alone. He let it rip, "Meanwhile back in Paris, I was embarrassed, B-a-a-a-a-be."

The drive was quick, and he soon arrived at headquarters. Despite his mild fluster over working with a new partner, the music had relaxed him. As he strode quickly down the long hallway, a quick glance at his watch told him he was actually early—in fact, too early. He slowed his pace and headed in the direction of the coffee room.

He hung his coat on a hook and retrieved his mug from the cupboard. Looking around the small room, he was surprised how drab it was. Maybe his time away had changed his perspective, or more likely it was because this morning he was the lone occupant. The room normally housed a raucous group of coffee-guzzling cops, making it the most lively and colourful place you could find.

Alone though, he noticed the grey walls, and how the stainless steel sink had lost its lustre, replaced with a permanent layer of brown coffee stain. A small fridge and a few tables and steel grey fold-up chairs were the only furnishings. There were no windows. Steve noticed a picture of the city's skyline hung crooked on the far wall. Someone must have decided the room could use some life and had hung it. The photo was now outdated and faded. Hanging askew, it proved to do anything but enliven its surroundings. Yes, he decided, the usual loud conversations and the camaraderie were what truly gave the room the warmth and charm he was accustomed to.

He headed to the coffee pot, only to find it empty. He quickly put on a pot and paced impatiently, waiting for it to brew. Finally, he could wait no longer. He poured himself a cup from the half-ready pot. He hated to do it, knowing it would mess up the rest of the pot. He sat down and wrapped his hands around the warm cup and decided, today, he didn't care.

The morning paper was on the table, and Steve skimmed the front-page headlines before flipping to the sports section. He wished he hadn't arrived quite so early. Having trouble concentrating on the paper, he put it down and instead, contemplated how he and his new partner would work out. He had met Grant Mayne once already and he had seemed like a decent guy. But it was not whether he'd like Grant that worried him. It was how Grant would feel about working with him. Steve knew some of the other detectives had found him difficult. He chuckled at that understatement. They liked him well enough; it was just a consensus that he was too meticulous—overboard was the word they often used—and worse. Working a crime scene with him could strain the most patient. Steve didn't care. It meant more to him to solve a case than win a popularity contest. Plus, his track record spoke for itself, Chief Dan could attest to that.

"You're early."

Steve looked up to see Chief Dan already pouring himself a cup of coffee. "Yeah."

"Grant here yet?"

"Haven't seen him"

"When he gets here I want to see you both in my office."

"Sure thing."

"And Steve…"

"What?"

"Don't look so damn worried. Grant's a good detective, so are you. You'll work well together."

"I know. Thanks."

Leaving the coffee room, Chief Dan took a sip of his coffee and made a sour face. "Who made this coffee, tastes like dishwater!"

Steve smirked, picked up the paper and was actually able to read it this time. Just as he became immersed in an article someone else came in the room.

"Morning, Steve."

It was Grant. What Grant lacked in height he more than made up for in bulk. He was stocky and solid. His shirt barely contained the muscles bulging on his arms. He was young. Steve figured somewhere in his mid to late 20s. He carried himself with confidence. Steve liked that.

Steve got up to shake Grant's hand, but as he did the back leg of his chair crossed the chair next to him and caused them both to clatter to the floor. The falling chairs echoed loudly in the stark coffee room. Grant chuckled and helped Steve pick up the chairs. So much for making a good first impression, Steve thought. "Boss wants to see us," was all he could manage.

Grant slapped Steve, hard, on the back. "Better go, then."

As they headed down the hallway they passed several uniforms. They all seemed to know Grant well and greeted him enthusiastically, some with jeering and laughter. It was obvious they all liked him. When they saw Steve they simply nodded an acknowledgement and quickened their step. Steve realized it was a long time ago when he was part of this young group of uniforms. All of a sudden he felt old.

As they passed the interrogation room Steve remembered the many times he had been in that room, unfortunately on both sides of the table. The most prevalent was the day he had shot and killed that low-life Jim Kobac. It had marked the beginning of an end for him, starting with his departure from the force, and then his nose-dive down a bottle of vodka. He had wanted to leave the force all together, but Chief Dan had convinced him to only take a leave of absence. The chief couldn't quite get why Steve was leaving at all. He had been cleared for duty, so there was no problem. Everyone knew he had shot Jim in self-defence, and the video had confirmed it.

When Steve left the force he was sure it was for good, but life has a way of surprising people, especially the ones living it. And now he knew this was where he belonged, so here he was again, back on the job.

When they arrived in Dan's office both Steve and Grant sat in the seats indicated for them. Chief Dan's office was a welcome respite from the coffee room. On his desk were several framed pictures of his family, and a large glass bowl full of butterscotch candies. Grant reached over and picked up an empty soup can that held an assortment of pens. As he did, a piece of macaroni was dislodged off the can and he grimaced. It was not just any soup can; it was decorated with, now faded, construction paper and macaroni. Crayon printing declared Chief Dan as, The World's Greatest Dad!

Grant tried unsuccessfully to stick the piece of macaroni back on. He looked up at Chief Dan, who simply shook his head, no. Grant put the can down carefully and placed the macaroni piece beside it. "Sorry, Chief."

Chief Dan slowly brushed back his grey hair with one strong, weathered hand. He lifted his coffee cup to his careworn face, took a big sip and then made a face. The coffee was bad to begin with, but now had gone cold. He took off his reading glasses and set them on the desk and looked at Steve and Grant. A smile formed.

"Well, if it isn't Holmes and Watson."

"Who?"

"I believe he's comparing us to the famous Sherlock Holmes and his sidekick Watson," Steve explained.

"I've seen that show, but wait a minute, Watson's a woman. I must be Sherlock then?"

Chief Dan sighed. "Let's move on. Grant. I want you to help Steve in his transition back to the street. He's been away a while, but he's one of the best. His style is quite different from your own 'get-'er-done' attitude, but I believe the two of you will complement each other."

Grant nodded.

"And Steve, let's just take it slow, one day at a time, OK?"

"Sure," Steve said.

"OK boys, I want you to continue with the investigation of the young man who was beaten to death in his own neighbourhood. Grant, bring Steve up to speed on that one before you head out."

"Will do."

"I've actually been studying up on that one already," Steve said. "Suspected gang ties, right?"

"Yeah, so watch your back. Now, get out of here."

CHAPTER THREE

Penny Clark yanked the covers over her face. Once again, the sun rose before her and was now blinding her eyes. She knew she was doomed to get up. As hard as she was to wake up, once she was, it was a useless effort for her to try to go back to sleep. The giant bed didn't help; without Steve, she felt very small and lonely in it.

As she stumbled out of bed she almost tripped over the grey sweats and T-shirt she had been wearing the night before. She considered putting them back on, but instead grabbed Steve's housecoat off the hook and put that on. It was long on her, and wrapped around her lithe body almost twice. It felt good. She secretly loved it, and wore it whenever Steve was out. It also held his aroma. She held a piece of it to her face and inhaled deeply.

Penny still lived with her parents. But when Steve went back to his old job, and rented this apartment, she found she was spending more and more time here. She used the excuse that it was quiet, conducive to her writing. The truth was she felt more at home here with Steve than she had ever felt anywhere. And that scared her.

She headed straight to the bathroom and smiled at how orderly it was. Even the faucets glittered. There was no maid, of course. Steve always wiped things down, even when he was in a hurry.

Penny brushed her teeth. She had always been told she had a nice smile, and at some point began to believe it. What she didn't like was how her smile accentuated her one big dimple deeply embedded on her left cheek. She thought it made her look too juvenile, less womanly. Her smattering of freckles didn't help much either. She threw some water on her face and quickly ran a brush through her hair. She surveyed her appearance briefly in the mirror. Her vibrant green eyes stared back at her. They always served to reassure her.

Slipping her feet into Steve's slippers, she shuffled into the kitchen to pour a cup of coffee. There was none. She sighed, and imagined Steve must have been in a real hurry this morning; he usually always put coffee on. She began making a fresh pot, and remembered that it was his first day working with his new partner, that Grant guy. She stood at the counter waiting for it to brew and then chose to take advantage of the pause-and-serve feature. She was anxious to get to work.

To Penny, her work was not work at all—it was her passion. It began at the Marlborough Hotel, where she used to work at the front desk. You couldn't work there without knowing about the resident ghost, Edith. Back in the '40s, Edith, just a young girl, had been murdered in the hotel, and many claimed she remained as a ghostly presence. Edith's spirit at the hotel was never really considered evil, but more of an innocent prankster who liked to monkey with the elevators. Even so, Penny wanted no part of it, and rarely ventured far from the front desk. At least she didn't until Steve started working security at the hotel, and all the havoc that ensued spun her into a whirlwind of events, including working with Steve to solve a murder.

Once she was catapulted beyond her post, and away from her paperback novels, Penny became more and more intrigued by Edith's story, past and present. That was the beginning of her fervour for local ghost stories. From the Marlborough ghost the next natural place for her to research was the Hotel Fort Garry, an infamously haunted entity.

Admittedly her research often gave her the jitters, but fascination always overruled her fear, and she continued. She literally held her breath as she read about the cloaked ghost of a woman and the legend of Room 202 at the Hotel Fort Garry. A young bride-to-be, Nadine, had hung herself in the closet after learning her fiancé had been killed in a car accident. According to the story, she was so overwhelmed by despair that she took her own life in hopes of joining him in death. Penny learned that many guests in Room 202 claimed to see her—a lost, mournful woman, floating over the foot of the bed, ever searching. Others saw her crying in the lounge. It seemed suicide did not work, and so Nadine's ghost persisted.

Penny settled in on the couch with her cup of coffee. Her laptop sat on the coffee table where she had left it the night before, and just looking at it made her smile. She remembered the day Steve had given it to her and how he had suggested that instead of reading so many, she should maybe consider writing a book. Initially, she had scoffed at the idea, until she learned the fateful story of Nadine. She was compelled to write Nadine's story, Edith's story, and others. She felt this might somehow give their life some meaning and hopefully give their souls some rest. She decided to try. Now here she was, already on chapter nine of her first book, and it was all thanks to Steve.

As anxious as she had been to get to work she lingered with her thoughts of Steve. He was a good man; at times this was his failing. She remembered when they had first met at the Marlborough. He himself was a lost soul, and as they became friends she longed to help him get over whatever it was that was dragging him down. It wasn't easy. Steve was not forthcoming on the subject of why he had left his job in homicide. When she finally found out, she realized why. It tore him, not knowing for sure if he had shot and killed Jim Kobac in self-defence, or whether he had actually taken the law into his own hands. She was so relieved when he finally came to terms with the truth everyone else had known for a long time. Penny didn't need any convincing on the matter.

Penny set her coffee on the end table, and then remembering, quickly placed a coaster under it. She wrapped his housecoat around herself a bit tighter and tucked her legs under herself on the couch. She considered how different Steve and she were. She had never thought of herself as messy, but in comparison to Steve, she sure was. She wondered how he put up with her. Then she smiled and remembered the night, and then she could imagine why.

It was true they differed in many ways. He was fearless. She on the other hand could be spooked by her own shadow. She rationalized that a homicide detective, with his training and type of job, had to have at least a modicum of bravery to his character.

She had been surprised how much she had grown to trust Steve. This was a miracle in itself considering her prior relationships. She had married young and thought that was it, till death do they part. When she caught him cheating she was hurt. When he said the affair meant nothing, she was devastated. She couldn't comprehend how he could risk everything they had for an affair that meant nothing. The guy she met after that was more of the same.

So she had resigned herself to the fact that she would never be in a relationship again. Why bother? Why set herself up to be hurt again? Then Steve showed up for work that day at the Marlborough Hotel. He was definitely handsome, with captivating eyes, and very tall. That was not what had drawn her in. It was his inconsistencies. His strong, rugged features and looming stature were in direct contrast to the story his eyes told. They spoke of forlornness and regret. This is what had aroused her curiosity and eventually reined her in. They were friends first, partners in solving crimes, then at some point it became more, much more, probably before either of them would admit it. Now she was scared to ever let him go.

They never discussed their relationship. It all seemed to happen so fast, and now they had this unspoken commitment to each other. She had never had the time, or liberty, to consider the relationship, to decide. It just happened. And that was OK, most of the time, but at other times it scared the hell out of her and she wondered how it had happened.

What scared her was that it would disappear, go wrong somehow. It would have been fine before, never knowing such fulfillment. Now that she did, she knew she couldn't survive without it. Spending her life with her nose in a book, enjoying her own company wasn't enough anymore. Life with Steve was vibrant. It made her feel alive. Neither had said it out loud, but they both knew it, they were in love. It was an unspoken fact they couldn't ignore.

Deciding she had squandered enough time daydreaming, she promised herself to get to work. She would just refill her coffee cup and get busy. With cup in hand she wandered into the kitchen—and then stopped dead in her tracks.

Penny screamed. The counter was awash in coffee. So was the floor! To her dismay, she realized that she hadn't replaced the coffee pot properly and it had continued to brew and spill everywhere. It was even dripping into the drawer she had left open. She frantically pulled reams of paper towels off the roll and began to soak up the mess. The phone began to ring loudly.

"Oh crap!"

She tried to ignore it and continue cleaning, but it kept ringing, so she threw the whole roll of paper towels on the worst of it and ran to grab the phone.

"Hello!" she blurted.

"Penny?"

CHAPTER FOUR

Thursday, February 13, 1947

It was positively perfect. Nadine was seated at the vanity, marvelling at her own reflection. The exquisite white cloak draped over her shoulders was the main source of her delight. Without taking her eyes away for a second, she carefully lifted the hood and rested it gently over her bouncy blond curls. With only her slip on underneath, she tried to imagine how wonderful it would all come together the next day. Carefully, she applied some rich red lipstick. She smiled glamorously and batted her long lashes as she rose to her feet. Taking a spin on one foot, she watched adoringly as the cloak floated in the air. It almost appeared as if she floated too.

Nadine was truly on Cloud 9. Tomorrow she would become Mrs. William Treadwill, and what an elegant affair it would be! She had always expected she might have a spring wedding, with a bouquet of lily of the valley. But when Bill had proposed at Christmas, neither of them could wait. Besides, who needed lily of the valley when you could have luscious red roses?

She continued to twirl around the room. It was only when she reached the bed that she stopped and the smile faded from her face.

She stood still. The bed was perfectly made and smelled of crisp and clean. Bending to run her hand over the bedspread, she tried to imagine what her wedding night would be. A feeling of anticipation, as well as apprehension, consumed her. It would be her first time. A large tear welled up in the corner of her eye and slowly rolled down her cheek. A rush of loneliness and uncertainty overcame her.

What was wrong with her? This attitude would not do! Before the dispiriting mood could draw her in any further, Nadine quickly brushed the tear off her cheek and willed herself to dismiss such thoughts. Forcing the smile back on her face, she moved away from the bed and headed toward the window. Arms outstretched, she gazed out. The night was mostly dark, with the exception of the white fluffy snowflakes drifting to the ground. Enchanted by them, she resumed twirling around the room in her beautiful cloak. The snowflakes appeared to follow her lead and began to swirl as well. Some of the flakes blew and hit the window straight on, as if wanting to come in and join her in her dance. It was to no avail; upon contact with the glass they would quickly melt to oblivion, gone forever.

Nadine remembered the first time she met Bill. He was very tall, at six foot three, some might say too tall, yet he never slumped. He carried his height proudly. William, or Bill as everyone called him, had the dreamiest dark eyes. They had enchanted her, yes, but it was truly his big toothy smile and his deep resounding voice that had proved to charm her beyond her wildest imagination. They had met at the picture shows, introduced by mutual friends. In retrospect, they suspected their meeting was not so much by chance, but more likely a carefully staged setup by well-intentioned friends.

After the show, a group of them had stopped in at The Chocolate Shop. The place was famous for the generous dollops of whipped cream that crowned every cup of hot chocolate. For Nadine and Bill it was yet another crowning glory to what was turning into a perfect evening. Nadine couldn't remember ever talking so much, yet Bill had done his fair share too. They talked so long they barely noticed when their friends had left. Finally, the owner had to ask them to settle their bill so he could close up and go home. Lingering and still smiling, Bill paid and left a generous tip. He helped Nadine on with her sweater and they left hand in hand. They had been inseparable ever since.

Until now…

As she sat alone in the room, Nadine couldn't help but reminisce about all their moments together. Oh, how she missed him! She had begged him not to go to Toronto. It was too close before the wedding, but Bill had gently insisted. The wedding had been only two weeks away and she had pleaded with every argument and used all the feminine wiles she could muster to convince him. Finally, he had to tell her point blank: it was business, and it was important, and she may as well learn to accept that now. Otherwise, he told her, they would not have the means to afford the luxuries they both enjoyed. She knew he was right, but pouted anyway.

Later, he had apologized for his sternness and presented her with a gift. The gift was beautiful, even before she opened it. It came in a glossy, white box, secured with a red velvet ribbon. Inside was the stunning cloak she now wore. It was made of white velvet and hosted a delicate fur-lined hood. She had gasped when she opened it, and she recovered quickly from her sulking.

She supposed that this gift, plus a wedding reception at the Hotel Fort Garry, no less, should make any girl happy for the rest of her life. The gift did appease her, but only for a while. With their wedding the very next day, she needed to see him, needed his reassurance. Where was he? Why did he have to go!

Sitting again at the vanity Nadine released a heavy sigh, picked up the telephone and dialed the front desk. A quiet young man answered.

"Good evening, this is Nadine Clyde in Room 202. Please tell me, has there been a message left for me?"

"I believe not, Miss Clyde, but let me check the register to be certain."

Nadine watched her reflection in the mirror as she waited. Noticing an unruly brow, she moistened the tip of her ring finger with her tongue and smoothed it into place. While doing so she caught a glimpse of her diamond engagement ring glittering in the reflection. The site of it reminded her of the promise of a new life. It calmed her and made her realize how silly she was being. Bill would be back soon; there was nothing to worry about.

"Miss Clyde, are you there?

Nadine returned her attention to the phone. "Yes, I am here."

"I have checked the register and, I am sorry Miss Clyde, there are no messages at this time."

"Oh...OK, well thank you for checking."

"Shall I ring you if one arrives?"

"Yes, please do that," she said, and then she added, "no matter what the hour."

She stood and removed her cloak. She draped it carefully over one arm, and headed toward the closet, where she hung it carefully right next to her wedding gown. She would have rather kept it wrapped around her, it was so warm, but she was afraid it would become creased or ruined in some way.

The closet was draughty, and a shiver rushed over her body. It made her think of an old superstition from her mother. When you shivered, she said, it meant someone had walked over your grave. Nadine was not a girl to let silly superstitions dictate her life. That's why she had insisted Bill come to see her as soon as his train arrived. When he cautioned her that it was bad luck to see the bride the night before the wedding, she replied it would be worse luck not to see him. She reached up and retrieved the extra blanket from the upper shelf of the closet and went to wait for him.

She settled in on the large wing chair facing the window, nestled her head on a soft pillow and tucked the warm blanket around her. She was not a believer in good luck or bad, but Nadine did believe wholeheartedly in rotten luck. She had had her share of it already. That was all behind her now. Everything had changed since she met Bill. She couldn't wait for him to arrive. It would be a brief meeting, of course. He would have to stay in his own room. Well, that night, anyway. Mesmerized by the falling snow out the window, Nadine drifted off to a sound sleep.

A loud knocking on the door jarred Nadine from her sleep. The abrupt awakening caused her to take a moment to recall exactly where she was. It wasn't the rooming house. No, it was the room at the Hotel Fort Garry. The one Bill had reserved for her...

The knocking became louder and more insistent.

The pillow dropped to the floor and the blanket was flung into the air. Nadine practically flew out of the chair.

"Bill, darling, you're back!"

CHAPTER FIVE

Monday, November 18, 2013

Grant and Steve headed to the conference room to review the case Chief Dan had assigned them. Grant held a folder with all the details and cleared his throat.

Before Grant could say anything Steve piped in, "So what we know is that the victim suffered injuries from a beating that led to his death." Steve pointed to the address on Grant's open folder, and then he continued. "Not the best neighbourhood, either, I know that area well. Used to be an OK place to live, not anymore. Today it's all about gangs. They own that area."

Grant tried to get in a word; after all it was he who was supposed be filling Steve in. "You're right Steve, the gangs run that area."

Before Grant could elaborate, Steve started up again. "I saw that you interviewed a witness. I bet there were more."

Steve continued on and on, reviewing every detail of the case without ever looking through the folder.

Grant wasn't sure if he was impressed or pissed.

"Well, Steve, I think I've sufficiently brought you up to speed on the case."

Grant's sarcasm was nearly lost on Steve.

"Oh I get it, good one. Sorry, but I just did a lot of pre-work on this one." Steve shrugged his shoulders and smiled. "My first case back and all; I guess I'm a bit keen."

"Keen?" Grant laughed. "Is that even a real word people use today?"

Grant expected to spend most of the morning reviewing the case, but with Steve already so thoroughly informed they were on the road by 11.

At Steve's insistence, they had decided to re-question the lady who witnessed the beating. Grant said she had been pretty tight-lipped at the initial interview, and despite her smart-ass attitude he could tell she was too scared to say much of anything. He couldn't blame her. Steve suggested that perhaps her memory was coming back, or the lapse of time may have made her a little less jumpy.

As they turned off Main Street and down the street to their destination, Steve noticed how badly rundown it had become, even worse than he remembered. The homes were mostly two-story and had been built too close together. They were old houses, and most had deteriorated. Broken and boarded-up windows, collapsed front steps and littered front lawns predominated. It was a shame, Steve thought; these homes could still be beautiful, and if kept up, a showcase of the past. Large elms lined on both sides of the street stood homage over the neighbourhood.

Gang signs on mailboxes, stop signs, and even on a few houses made it obvious who ruled the area. These graffiti artists were no Banksys. You couldn't really call their black, spray-painted, indiscernible shapes art. They were more of a symbol with the sole purpose to mark the territory.

There were few to no people on the sidewalks or in the yards. Curtains and blinds were drawn tightly. It was eerily quiet. The detectives left their car. Grant pulled a small piece of paper with the house number, 537, and began reviewing the front doors.

He shook his head when he saw Steve already negotiating a decaying sidewalk to the front door of the house marked 537.

Like all the houses on the street, it was old. This one had one of those huge, screened-in front porches. Steve hated them. He never knew whether to knock from the outside door or go into the porch and knock from there, and usually ended up doing both. After banging on the outside door a few times, with no response, they decided to go into the porch. Just before they did, Steve noticed a young kid, about 12, watching them from the other side of the street. He was on a bike and when he saw that they had noticed him, he sped toward the back lane.

As they entered the porch Steve looked around. It was dismal. It had the potential for a nice sitting area, but it was nothing of the sort. Instead it was a mournful pile of debris. A big chair sat in one corner with its stuffing oozing out of several rips. Its cushion had a large stain and rested on the floor beside it. Stacks of beer empties, some broken, gave the room a stale odour. At the other end of the porch was an old wooden toboggan that had seen better days. They stepped over a broken beer bottle to knock on the second door.

After waiting some time a woman finally came to the door, opening it just a crack. Her hair was a mess and her eyes were merely red slits. She looked at them curiously, but didn't speak, or invite them in.

"Morning, I'm not sure…"

She opened the door a little wider and leaned her head out towards them. "Go away," she whispered.

Steve thought this might be a good time to introduce himself and state their purpose. Before he had the chance, a very large, angry-looking man came out of the bedroom and swung open the door. The woman backed away. The man wore jeans but no shirt. He had a lot of tattoos.

He stood in the doorway, as if to block their entrance, and stretched one arm out, resting it high on the frame. It was then that Steve noticed a strange little tattoo on the guy's wrist. He couldn't miss it. It was practically in his face. It looked like a spider, yes. It was. A red spider with a skull for a face. Steve frowned.

"You got a warrant?"

"No sir, we just wanted to—"

"Get the fuck out of my house."

The man turned to walk back to the bedroom then stopped and looked over his shoulder, straight at Grant. Letting out a malicious laugh he went into the bedroom and shut the door. The woman just stood there, staring into space.

Grant motioned with an impatient tilt of his head for them to get going. Steve would have rather pressed on to talk to the woman, but Grant was already walking away. Frustrated, Steve followed and then figured maybe Grant was right, they had no warrant, they couldn't very well just barge their way in for no good reason. Plus, he didn't want to cause trouble with his partner on the first day working together, so he let Grant take the lead on this one.

"Well it was worth a try," Grant said.

"Yeah. Hey, did you notice that kid on the bike earlier?"

"Yeah, I did."

"I have a hunch he might know something, just the way he looked at us."

"Steve, we can't just go interrogating every kid on the street. Besides, I'm hungry."

Grant pulled out a credit card and started to clear some ice that had settled on the windshield. Steve made a mental note to get him a proper scraper.

"I really think we should talk to him," Steve said.

"Nah, let's just go for lunch. We're not going to solve this one your first morning out."

"OK, OK, but just give me five minutes. Let's just go see if he's still around. Find out who he is." Steve wasn't letting up on this one.

Grant let out a heavy sigh, as if now realizing what the other's meant when they talked about Steve's meticulousness.

Just then Grant's cellphone rang. Glancing apologetically at Steve, he fumbled to get his cell out of his pocket. As he did so he looked at Steve and said, "OK, OK, five minutes, we'll go find the kid. I'm right behind you."

Steve began walking toward the back lane.

Grant spoke into his cell. "Hello... no, not now, I'll call you later."

The caller was not dismayed and continued trying to keep Grant's attention.

Steve saw the kid was there, but he wasn't alone. Another kid, maybe a bit older, was with him. It looked like they were exchanging something. Steve walked up to them and they both looked up. They looked scared.

"Hi guys, what's up?"

The older kid turned and ran.

"Come back here!"

Steve was just about to take chase when he felt an excruciating pain in his upper thigh. As he fell over he watched the younger kid jump on his bike. He saw him throw a bloody pocketknife into the snow.

Grant had shoved the cell back in his pocket. It was ringing again, but he ignored it in his hurry to catch up to Steve. It had only been a minute or so, but you never let your partner go alone, even to talk to a kid, not in this neighbourhood.

The minute or so had been all it took. Steve was lying in a pool of blood. The young kid was pedalling away as fast as he could. Grant rushed over to Steve. First he pulled out his cellphone and called in. He told the dispatch they had an officer down, and quickly gave their location.

His first aid training kicked in. He assessed the area for safety and that is when he noticed the bloody knife in the snow. The kid was long gone, so he concentrated on Steve's injury. It was a knife puncture— small, but he was losing blood quickly and that could be dangerous, if not fatal. Grant was going to use his jacket to stop the blood from flowing when he remembered a trick he'd heard of. As he recalled, you place the card over the wound to cover it completely. You were then supposed to tape it down, leaving one corner unsealed to prevent a pressure buildup. He obviously didn't have any tape so he would just have to hold it and apply pressure. The knife had ripped Steve's pants at entry, but the rip wasn't big enough, so Grant quickly ripped the pants more, enough to cover the wound with the credit card. Then he grabbed his credit card that was thankfully still in his pocket from scraping the windows. He covered the wound and hoped it worked. It did. It actually seemed to be stopping the blood flow. Steve had already lost too much blood, and he was looking pretty weak.

How the hell could this happen? He wanted to chase the little bastard, but knew his priority was to take care of Steve. As he held the credit card in place he looked toward the houses around him, hoping for some help. It may as well have been a ghost town. He was sure he saw the curtains moving in the window of the house directly behind them, but that was it.

"You'll be just fine Steve, help's on the way. It's just a little nick."

"Call Penny," Steve said weakly.

Then Steve's eyes rolled back and he was out.

"Oh shit," Grant said. Then he heard the sirens. "Hurry, please hurry. Come on."

CHAPTER SIX

Penny stood there holding the phone, irritated that it had interrupted her. Steve would have a fit if he knew about the coffee mess she had made.

"Penny?"

"Yes?"

"It's Chief Dan. Listen, Steve's been hurt. I'm really sorry I don't have any details yet. Come to Health Science Centre Emergency. Don't drive. There's an officer in front of your building waiting for you."

She dropped the phone.

It was as if her world had crashed to a stop. She moved about quickly, but perceived it all in slow motion. She thought she might throw up. Instead, she focused all her efforts on concentrating on what had to be done. She threw on her sweatpants and T-shirt from the day before, slipped into a pair of boots and then grabbed a long jacket out of the closet as she ran out the door. An officer met her in the apartment lobby. He gestured for her to come with him. He put his strong arm over her shoulder to guide her. She felt she might crumple to the ground at any moment.

The officer opened the back door of the patrol car for her to get in. Penny sat there like a wounded bird. She wanted to just let it all out, but she knew if she did, she wouldn't be able to stop. Instead, she sat herself up straight and asked the officers what they knew of Steve's condition.

"Well, I guess Chief Dan told you he'd been stabbed by some kid."

Penny gasped. She forced herself to steady her breathing. She would deal with the emotions later. Right now she had to concentrate.

"No, he didn't. How bad was it?"

"We're not sure at this point, but we do know his partner called for help immediately then proceeded with administering first aid. I'm sure he'll be fine."

"Thank you, please hurry."

The driver switched on the siren and accelerated.

It wouldn't take long to get to the hospital. Steve's apartment at The Towers was downtown, and the hospital wasn't very far from there. Yet, for Penny, it seemed the longest drive of her life.

All the way, all she could focus on was Steve. She thought about the day before, Sunday. It hadn't been anything special, but they had spent most of it together so it was. They had gone out for dim sum. She loved dim sum, but never really knew what to order. She was totally at his mercy for their selections. The carts of Chinese delicacies zipped around at a fast pace, with the servers pausing briefly at each of the packed tables. Steve politely declined most of them, but always seemed to know which ones to stop, to select their favourites. Shrimp dumplings and sticky rice were always a must. Some of the dishes were beyond their simple tastes, and Penny was glad he never wanted to get too adventurous.

Yesterday, though, she had gone to the ladies room, and when she returned to the table a fresh bamboo basket had been set at her place. She sat down, still hungry, and went to remove the lid. Then she saw chicken feet poking out of the bamboo basket. She was furious until she saw Steve trying to stifle his laugh. Once she laughed, so did Steve. She told him that it was a terrible thing to do and the only way she'd forgive him was if he'd eat one. He did, but just the one.

The rest of the day was spent in the apartment. She worked on her book and pretty much ignored him. The only time they really had spoken was when she wanted his opinion. He always obliged with honest comments. Her book was a story about the ghost that is said to haunt the Hotel Fort Garry, and she was thoroughly enjoying writing it. She was so grateful Steve had encouraged her to begin writing, but was sorry, now, that she had paid so little attention to him. Then she remembered she had… later.

Oh Steve, she thought. God, please let him be OK, please let him be OK.

The car pulled up to the emergency entrance. The officer in the front passenger seat got out and opened the back door for her. She nearly knocked him over as she jumped out and ran toward the door. He noticed, and wondered at, a trail of red tartan dragging from the back of her coat.

CHAPTER SEVEN

Thursday, February 13, 1947

Nadine flung open the door and flashed her biggest smile, and then stood frozen in the doorway. Her smile held, but her brow furrowed as her head tilted. Instead of her fiancée, she was met with two sombre police officers. For just a moment, it was as if time had stopped.

Both officers stared, despite themselves. All she had on was her white slip. They averted their eyes quickly to maintain an official presence, but their blush of embarrassment belied the façade. One officer stared at his shuffling foot, as if it were the most interesting thing in the world. The other looked up towards the ceiling. It was only then that Nadine realized her inappropriate state of dress.

Finally, the officer staring at the ceiling spoke. "Miss Clyde?"

"Yes, come in." She ran and grabbed the blanket off the floor and covered herself. She was the one staring now. Her mind would not work; she could not sort out their purpose for coming to her door. She surmised it must be some kind of mistake.

"Are you Miss Nadine Clyde, fiancée to Mr. William Treadwill?"

The question gave her a familiar thrill, and she answered proudly, "Yes, I am."

The officer hesitated, and then just said it. "I'm afraid there's been a terrible accident."

Nadine's heart began to sink. Her body tensed while every fibre of her being was on alert, and yet she felt she couldn't move, as if moving would make the moment progress. Pausing, she brushed a loose blond curl that had fallen over one eye, and then spoke slowly.

"What kind of accident?

She watched as both officers exchanged looks of despair. She wished she could just fall back and faint, escape what was to follow. She did not. Instead, she sat herself down slowly into the wing chair. She held both arms stiff as she lowered herself down. The room was silent.

She asked in a barely audible whisper, "Is it Bill?"

Then she stood defiantly. "Is he OK? Of course he is. I think you've made a mistake."

"We regret to inform you that Mr. William Treadwill was struck by a motor car on Main Street at approximately 9:15 this evening."

Nadine stood tall and made her way to the window. With her back turned to them she advised them in no uncertain terms, "No, you're wrong. You've made a terrible mistake. Bill is coming here. He should be here any moment. We're getting married tomorrow."

Nadine was now terrified, but masked it with anger. How dare they come here and tell her such lies.

"We're sorry, miss. There is no mistake. The driver said he came out of nowhere. A witness claims he had dashed out onto Main Street after leaving the train station. It was snowing quite heavy, miss. I don't believe the driver, nor Mr. Treadwill, ever saw each other coming—until it was too late."

The news was sinking in. Nadine stood and went over to the dressing table. She ran a brush through her curls and quickly applied some lipstick. Grabbing a tissue, she wiped away a determined tear and willed herself to maintain her composure.

"If you'll just give me a moment to dress, I'll need a ride to the hospital to see him, please."

The officers just stood there, not moving.

Nadine flung open the closet door. "He is at the hospital, right? This is just terrible. I suppose we'll have to postpone the wedding now. Oh well, the important thing is that Bill is all right."

Just as she was about to grab her beautiful cloak out of the closet, she heard the words.

"I'm so sorry, he didn't survive, miss. I regret to tell you he died on impact. He wouldn't have even known what happened."

The other officer added, "You can take solace that he didn't suffer."

Nadine stood facing the inside of the draughty closet, her back to the officers. She did not turn around as she addressed them. "Thank you gentlemen, can you please leave now?"

They both hesitated, not moving.

"Is there someone we can call?"

"No, thank you, I'm fine. Please, I would like to be alone now."

After a long pause, she sensed they weren't planning on leaving. She turned and looked directly at them. She even smiled briefly to convince them she would be fine.

"We don't like to leave you alone after such a shock."

"I'm fine, really."

When they continued to hesitate, Nadine let the blanket slip down her shoulders slightly, just enough to remind them how little she was wearing. Relenting hesitantly, the red-faced officers moved toward the door. In reality they were somewhat relieved to have permission to leave. They left a card with a number for her to call in the morning, and then tipped their hats and left, with a promise they would alert the front desk to check on her.

The last sound she heard was the loud click of the door as they shut it. She returned to the chair, and slumped into it. This time she did not bother with the blanket. She was unaware of how chilled her skin was or the fact that she was shivering uncontrollably. One lone snowflake fluttered briefly outside the window, then floated up past her view and disappeared.

CHAPTER EIGHT

Monday, November 18, 2013

Chief Dan and Penny moved down the hospital corridor at a fast clip.

"How bad is he?"

"He's going to be OK, Penny. Had a knife wound to the leg, lost a lot of blood, but they got to him quick, I'm sure he'll be OK."

Their steps resounded loudly in lonesome echoes as they continued.

Chief Dan was supposed to be leading the way. He was the one who knew where Steve was, yet he found himself running behind her, shouting directions as they went. The twists and turns of the hospital corridors went on forever. Each looked the same as the last, but Chief Dan made sure he kept close attention the first time.

"Turn left at the elevators!" he shouted.

Penny began to run now and the chief did his best to keep up. He was out of breath when he pointed to a door that a nurse was just leaving. Penny pushed past the nurse and into the room.

There he was, lying in the bed.

His face looked ashen, but Penny was relieved to see his eyes were open—droopy, but open. The room's dimness was barely disturbed by the lights from several monitors. One beeped intermittently. Penny let out a long breath, one she felt she had been holding ever since the phone rang with the terrible news. Chief Dan walked in behind her.

"Hello beautiful," Steve whispered when he saw her.

She ran to his side, carefully leaned over the bed and held her hand to his cheek and stroked it with her thumb.

"You'd better be talking to her and not me," said Dan in a futile attempt to lighten the moment.

The nurse poked her head in. "He's on a lot of medication, but he's still fairly lucid."

"I'm OK, Pen, don't worry."

"Well, you two don't need me here. I'll just be outside," Chief Dan said. No one seemed to hear or notice him, so he backed quietly out of the room.

Steve's eyes were closed now. Penny pulled up a chair beside his bed and just sat and stared at him. She smiled. Through it all, his hair was in perfect place. She always envied his thick, dark hair. She knew he was vain about it, even though he never said a word. She also knew he worried that his nose was too big. It wasn't. He was a very handsome man. It didn't seem right to see him lying in a hospital bed. His long, lean body was almost too big for the bed. Penny reached for his hand and held it. It felt cool, so she held it in both her hands to warm it. His eyes fluttered. She rested her cheek on the back of his hand and let the tears fall.

"Pen?"

She didn't want to upset him. She sat up straight, grabbed a tissue from the box sitting on the metal end table and wiped her eyes.

"I'm right here, Steve."

"I'm sorry."

"Sorry, for what?"

"Everything. For getting hurt, for loving you so much."

"You love me?"

The bed was too high to see him properly from the chair, so she stood. She put her face close to his and couldn't believe what she heard next.

"Course I do. How could I not? You're the best thing that ever happened to me. You are so beautiful and I…"

It was then that Penny remembered what the nurse had said. It was just the drugs talking. For a second there, she thought…

"Do you love me too, Pen?"

She hesitated, but only for a moment. "Sure, Steve, of course I do." She knew it was true, but only admitted it to him because of his condition.

"I don't know how you could. You are too beautiful. What are you doing with a guy like me?"

Penny smiled at this. Boy, would he be sorry he said that! "Maybe you should rest awhile."

"Marry me, Penny?"

"What?"

"I know you were hurt before, but come on, take a chance on us. Please marry me, Pen. I love you so much. I don't ever want to be without you."

Penny didn't know what to say. Fresh tears began to fall. If only he would have told her this before. Not now, delirious with the drugs. He probably won't even remember any of this, she thought.

"Sure Steve, I'll marry you. Now, get some rest."

He closed his eyes and fell asleep. Penny stood up and left the room.

CHAPTER NINE

Friday, February 14, 1947

Nadine had no idea how long she sat in the chair after the officers left. The phone rang a few times, but she could barely move, let alone get up to answer it. She went over it in her head over and over. How could it have all gone so wrong? She couldn't, wouldn't believe Bill was dead. It just couldn't be so! If he really were, what on earth would she do now? How could she ever live without him?

She thought back, remembering how lonely she had been, before she had met Bill, how hard it was when she had first moved to Winnipeg. She had loved living here, but things hadn't been going well for her, especially financially.

At one point she was certain she was going to have to go back home to the farm, and that was her worst fear. After her mother had died it was unbearable living with her father and her brothers. They were mean and demanding. She found out how hard her mother had worked, and it was not the life she wanted for herself; she just had to get away. When she told them she was leaving, her father forbade it. She chose to defy him and left late one night without a word.

With one small suitcase and a heart heavy with hope, she had set out on the long walk to town. It was a warm, clear evening, and the stars lit her way along the dark gravel road. Her suitcase held only a few meagre belongings, and a photo of her mother. She had snatched the photo off the piano before she left. In the picture her mother was young, a real beauty, not the farm-worn mother she knew. There was a guitar player in the background and a drummer, who was supposedly her father. Nadine couldn't fathom it. Her mother held a microphone and wore a sparkly dress. Nadine didn't feel bad bringing the picture, she knew her father never liked it on display, but Mom had insisted. Nadine often noticed her mother looking over at it with a wayward smile as she tended to her many chores.

With dust in her shoes and sand in her eyes, Nadine arrived in town just in time to catch the first bus to Winnipeg. Before she settled into her seat she removed the photo from her suitcase. She wondered at her mother's happiness captured on film, and silently promised to find her own.

With the photo on her lap, she slept most of the way. When the bus pulled into Winnipeg, the other passengers' chatter woke her. She was very excited as she peered out the dirty bus window. She licked her fingers and rubbed them on the window to get a clearer view. As the bus pulled into the depot, she was already on her feet, gripping her suitcase tightly. Once off the bus and inside the depot she ran to the first pay phone to call home. They would have been up for a while now, likely worried sick. She had to let them know she was OK! Her father hung up on her before she could even say where she was.

After a few months of living in Winnipeg, some of the excitement had worn off. Hunger had replaced hope. She wasn't starving, but many meals were skipped. Being so young, only 19, she often chose to spend her small paycheque from the pharmacy on new shoes, rather than groceries.

A knock at the door interrupted her thoughts. She could not will herself to rise to answer it.

The knocking became louder.

"Go away, please."

"Miss Clyde, are you OK?"

"Yes, please, I just need to be alone."

"I understand Miss Clyde. We've heard you received some unfortunate news."

She did not answer.

"We were worried. We rang you, but there was no answer."

"Please, I'm very tired."

"Yes, well, I promised the officers I'd check on you. Please let me know if you need anything at all."

"I will. Thank you."

She heard his footsteps diminish.

The conversation brought her back to the reality of her present circumstance. Here she was, all alone in their honeymoon suite, and Bill was never coming—he was dead! Hit by a motorcar! How ridiculous it seemed. This couldn't be real. Then a horrible thought presented itself: he was rushing to see her. He couldn't wait, and that was why he didn't look where he was going. Just as she was going to blame herself, she noticed the snow had started up again, this time with a fury. It swirled violently outside the window.

It was the damn snow! The motorcar couldn't see him because of the snow! Her hands curled into fists and her fingernails dug into her palms. Renewed strength consumed her as she rose and walked toward the window.

"It was the snow!"

CHAPTER 10

It turned out that Steve was OK. His pride was wounded much more than his leg. First day back on the streets and he was in the hospital before lunch. Put in by a kid, yet. He figured he'd never live it down.

Steve sat at his kitchen table, with one leg resting on a pillow Penny had put on a chair for him. His elbow relaxed with his face resting on his fist as he watched Penny intently. Her brow was furrowed as she glared at her Scrabble letters. She had once claimed to be the Scrabble Queen, and now, with time to kill, she had her big chance to prove it. He smiled at how seriously she took the game. Each of her turns was endless. She would shuffle her letters this way and that and then focus her gaze on the board. Steve learned quickly that he was not allowed to speak during her turn. He had tried, out of boredom; without even looking at him, Penny had held up her index finger and shushed him.

Steve had just smiled. It reminded him of the day they had met. It was his first day as security guard at the Marlborough Hotel. Penny had been working the front desk and was more interested in her paperback novel than letting his new boss know he had arrived. Although this had ruffled him, he couldn't help but notice how attractive she was.

At a quick glance, her petite frame and her blunt-cut brown hair might give her an average appearance. Look a little closer and you noticed a uniqueness that was her beauty. A deep dimple on one cheek and a smattering of freckles were interesting, but her luminous green eyes made her captivating. Later, Steve began to appreciate more bewitching aspects of her presence, like today as she sat in her jean cutoffs and a tight-fitting shirt. The outfit intensified her petite frame in all its understated curves, in particular her shapely, sensuous legs.

Normally she trudged around his place in that god awful grey sweat suit, but the thermostat in the apartment was malfunctioning and Steve was enjoying the heat. Made a guy want to flip a Scrabble board and, wounded leg be damned, chase her into the bedroom. Who was he trying to kid, even the damn sweat suit had a certain allure. When it came to Penny, no matter what she was wearing, or not wearing, she had quite an effect on him.

Penny looked at Steve. "Hello?"

"Hello!"

"It's your turn. Mark me down for a measly 12 points."

Steve chuckled. "All that time for 12 points, perhaps a new Scrabble King will be crowned today, huh?"

Penny ignored him while she picked out her next letters. When she looked up, Steve was already placing tiles on the board.

"Z–o–o, and that's on a triple-word score, 36 points for the soon-to-be Scrabble King!"

Penny checked it and he was right, 36 damn points. She sighed and Steve felt apologetic. He knew she would rather be working on her novel; without realizing it, she had glanced over at her laptop several times. He knew she was just trying to keep him occupied while he convalesced. It wasn't fair to beat her at her own game, at least under these circumstances.

"I could think of a lot more fun ways we could kill some time, can't you, Penny?" He dramatically raised his eyebrows up and down and smiled maliciously.

"Oh is that all you think of? You're wounded, for God's sake."

She smiled as she said it, though. She dumped her letters back in the box and made her way over to him.

Steve watched her come to him as he lifted his injured leg off the chair. Just as she reached to help him up, his cellphone rang. It was Chief Dan.

Penny stood beside him, waiting while he took the call. It was a short call. Steve hung up and looked up at her.

"I gotta go, Pen."

"Really! Why?"

"Chief Dan needs me to come in right away. They brought in the kid that did this." He pointed to his leg.

"Want me to drive you?"

"No, I can grab a cab. You probably want to get back to your writing…"

Penny was already heading into the other room to grab her laptop.

"OK, if you're sure."

Steve struggled with his crutches a bit more than necessary as he went out the door. Penny never noticed.

After he was gone, Penny stared at the blank screen of her laptop for a long time. As much as she wanted to get back to her writing, she found she couldn't concentrate. She couldn't help but wonder at how relieved she was that Steve was OK. The whole ordeal had been quite a shock for her and it had made her more scared than ever—scared of how much she loved him, scared it could end. She thought of all the things he had said at the hospital. He said he loved her too. He had even asked her to marry him! She knew it was just the drugs talking, and obviously he didn't remember a thing, and for that, she was grateful.

CHAPTER ELEVEN

"Where's the kid?"

Steve had burst into the coffee room, as fast as he could on his crutches. Grant was on his cell but quickly hung up. He looked up at Steve and smiled sheepishly.

"Glad you're OK, Steve. The kid's in the interrogation room."

"When can we talk to him?"

"Chief Dan told me to wait here for you. He'll come get us." Grant rose and pulled a chair out for Steve.

Steve sat down, feeling somewhat defeated.

"Pour me a cup of that sludge, would ya?"

Grant obliged, and then pulled up a chair across from Steve. There was no one else in the coffee room.

"Listen Steve, I feel awful. If I'd have been right with you"—he pointed at Steve's crutches—"this would have never happened."

"Whoa, Grant. Aren't you the guy who saved me? Nice trick with that credit card. Anyway, I was the one hell-bent on talking to the kid. All you did was answer your phone. I shoulda waited."

Just then Grant's cellphone rang again. He pressed a button to shut it off.

"You know Grant, you can tell me to mind my own business, but do you want to tell me who called you the day I got stabbed?"

"Oh it was Angel, my wife. She's got the face of an angel, all right, but she's a handful."

"Everything OK with you two?"

Steve didn't normally like to pry into anyone's personal business, but he knew that sometimes when working with a partner it was a good idea. It was a safety measure—for both of them.

"Oh yeah, we're good. You meet Angel, you'll see why I'm so crazy about her. She just quit her job, though, and is home a lot, and that gives her a lot of time to worry about me. That's why she's always calling."

"Well, you can understand that in your line of work. Why'd she quit her job?"

"Seems I'm not the only one who can't resist her. She was always complaining about guys she worked with hitting on her. I finally told her to quit. Money will be tight, but she wants to start a business. She's a smart one. If anyone can do it, she can."

Chief Dan poked his head into the coffee room. "Let's go."

With a one-hand wave he motioned for them to follow. Grant left quickly, and then came back to help Steve with his crutches. The three of them headed down the hallway to the interrogation room. Steve did his best to keep up.

Chief Dan slapped a file into Grant's hand and sat himself in a chair outside the window of the interrogation room. Running his hand through his thick grey hair, he leaned forward toward the window.

"You were right about the kid all along, Steve, he knows something," Grant said. He motioned for Steve to follow him into the room.

The first thing Steve noticed was that the kid looked nervous. It didn't help when Grant slapped the folder on the table and opened it to show a picture of the murder victim. It was a grim picture showing the badly beaten victim lying in a pool of his own blood. The kid looked away, fidgeting. Grant leaned over the table and outstretched his solid arms.

"Tell us what you know kid, now!"

Grant was in the kid's face and was not backing down. Steve could see what Chief Dan meant about Grant's get-her-done attitude. The kid looked down at the table in an attempt to avoid Grant's glare. This didn't work, Grant leaned his head on the table and looked up at the kid and demanded, "Look at me, and answer—NOW!"

Even though this was the kid that had stuck a knife in his leg, Steve was starting to feel sorry for him. He looked even younger than Steve remembered.

The kid fidgeted some more and focused his attention on a spider crawling on the table.

Grant smacked the spider until it was only a blotch.

That was when the kid talked.

Turns out the victim made a fatal mistake when he took a stroll in the wrong neighbourhood, wearing the wrong colours. The kid explained how the local gangs claim their territory and identify themselves by their colour of clothing. The victim had no gang ties, but just happened to be wearing the colours from a rival gang, and so appeared as a threat, a case of mistaken identity. It cost him his life and he didn't know why.

With the kid's information, they were able to identify a few suspects from the area. One was Jerome Stead, and neither Grant nor Steve was surprised to learn his address was the same as the house they had visited before, with the female witness who wouldn't talk. Jerome had to be the guy who sent them on their way when they didn't have a warrant, in the same neighbourhood where the kid had shoved a knife into Steve's leg.

Steve and Grant wasted no time in pursuing the lead, and left immediately. When their car pulled into the neighbourhood, dusk was setting in and the streetlights had come on. The large elms were illuminated, giving the worn-down neighbourhood a false beautification. If you looked closer you saw the rot and decay of the littered and neglected old homes.

When they arrived at Jerome's address they manoeuvred as quickly as they could over the decaying sidewalk. This time they didn't bother knocking on the front porch door, but went directly through to the inside front door. The man, Jerome answered the door. He was huge and took up most of the doorway. He wore a shirt that covered most of his tattoos. When he saw Steve and Grant he just laughed and tried to shut the door in their faces, but Steve forced himself in first.

"You assholes got a—"

He didn't have time to finish. Steve steadied himself with one arm firmly holding the door frame and grabbed Jerome's wrist and twisted it behind his back. Grant took over from there, pushing Jerome to the ground and cuffing him. Jerome was a big guy, and even in recovery with his leg wound Steve knew he had to take advantage of a surprise action. It worked.

Grant pulled Jerome up on his feet.

Steve looked him in the eye. "Yeah buddy, we got a warrant this time—an arrest warrant."

Jerome was one of only a few suspects, and Steve was really surprised when it turned out the guy had a solid alibi. In the end, with forensics and Steve's attention to detail, they charged three others. All of a sudden these tough guys were pleading for mercy, said they never meant to kill the guy, just wanted to teach him a lesson.

"Lessons aren't too helpful to dead guys," Steve told them. "I sure hope the courts teach you all a good one."

Grant and Steve were taught a lesson too. Now that the case was closed, Chief Dan asked to see both Steve and Grant. They both arrived in Chief Dan's office standing proud, expecting an 'atta boy' from the Chief. They got that and more. After telling them he was pleased with their work, that he knew he was right about pairing them up, he finally told them how he felt about the day Steve was stabbed. He told them it could have been a lot worse. How concerned he had been.

"You two are partners. That means you do things together. I don't care if it's a kid, a baby or a little old lady! You are a team, you always go in together!"

They both nodded. They knew he was right.

CHAPTER TWELVE

Friday, February 14, 1947

"It was the snow!"

Nadine's scream was maniacal, barely recognizable as human. She banged on the window with one hand, then the other, over and over again. Her clenched fists hit the panes harder and faster as tears streamed down her face. When the glass shattered, she barely noticed. She only continued. It grew easier, and soon she was pounding at nothing but a gaping hole. Blood spurt out of the gashes she had suffered from the broken shards. Rich crimson droplets fell on the snowy white sill. She felt no pain.

Defeated, she dropped her arms to rest, and watched the blood ooze from her wounds. Her tears ceased and she stood frozen, staring blankly beyond the window, toward the darkness.

When a blast of cold wind gusted through the broken window it roused her from the trance-like spirit that had overcome her, and returned a slight sense of awareness. Enough to make her remember. As the icy air swept through her, past her, she rose. A deathly chill gripped the once warm room. Gusts continued to blow, and soon swirls of snow followed.

Nadine went mad. She ran around the room, chasing the snow-flakes, cursing their very existence. To her dismay, they were fleeting, gone before she could derive the satisfaction of finishing them herself. Many blew toward the wall and rested momentarily. Nadine pressed her body against that wall and slammed her bare hands against it in utter despair. Once again, tears fell. Her blood splattered on the rose petal wallpaper and trickled lazily down the wall.

Squeezing her eyes shut, she prayed for it all to go away.

Finally, exhausted, she fell back onto the bed. As if on cue, the wind eased and the snow stopped blowing in. Nadine lay on the bed, blood still dripping, blemishing the once pristine bed. The room was quiet. She forced herself to think. Rational thoughts told her to call the front desk, ask for help, at the very least get up and wrap a towel over her wounds. She decided on the latter, but just as she was about to get up, her attention was drawn to the open closet. Her beautiful robe was hanging there, right beside her wedding dress—the dress she would now never wear. The site of it caused her to dismiss all sound reasoning and led her to a heart-wrenching decision.

"No…I will wear it!" Rising weakly from the bed, she went to the closet, retrieved her dress and carefully removed it from the hanger. She put it on slowly, taking care not to crumple the white lace skirt, despite the fact that it already embodied droplets of her own blood. The dress swished loudly as she crossed the silent room. She pulled out the stool and calmly sat herself down at the vanity. As she brushed her blond curls she hummed the Bridal Chorus, "Here comes the bride," and admired her reflection.

The room had taken on an icy chill from the broken window, blood had splattered and dripped everywhere, yet aside from this, the sight of Nadine humming and brushing her hair at the vanity could have been the scene of any young bride-to-be, blissfully preparing for her nuptials. That is, until she dipped her finger into her own coagulating blood and calmly applied it to her lips. It gleamed and glistened. A bright crimson on her full lips that actually proved to appear quite glamorous, until it began its macabre drool down the corners of her mouth. Nadine frowned at the site of this image; the image frowned back at her.

Rising from her seat, she turned her back to the mirror and resumed humming her song. She slowly dragged the stool from the vanity to the closet. She stood on it to reach for her beautiful white cloak. Bill had bought it for her, she remembered fondly. Removing its belt, she draped the cloak loosely over her shoulders. She tied the belt firmly to the rod in the closet and yanked it a few times to ensure its strength. Pushing the stool into the closet, Nadine turned and stepped backward onto the stool. Looping the dangling end of the belt firmly around her neck, she steadied her footing and discontinued her song.

With her eyes wide open, she stared toward the broken window and spoke in a hushed whisper. "I will never leave this room without you, Bill. I love you so."

With these words spoken, she proceeded quickly to kick the stool away.

CHAPTER THIRTEEN

Saturday, January 11, 2014

This winter in Winnipeg was more brutal than usual, bitterly cold with heavy snow. Steve hadn't missed that part of the job—braving the out-doors, scraping for evidence in the worst of conditions and driving on horrible roads. Plus, his leg was bothering him. Penny had noticed that his habit of tapping his thigh when anxious had now accelerated. As much as he liked being back on the job, he was glad it was Saturday, a day off, a day to just stay home.

Penny had other ideas. She wanted to do some research for her book, and it was time to face the ghosts head on. The only problem was she was terrified to go alone. It was Steve's day off, and when she asked him to come with her she noticed the tapping of his thigh first, and then the wince.

"Never mind!"

"What? I didn't say anything."

"You didn't have to."

Steve got up and went for his coat.

"Oh come on, you don't have to go. I know you don't want to."

While she said it, she also grabbed her own coat and they headed out.

After parking Steve's car in the front loop, they headed in. The wind practically blew them up the steps and through the revolving doors. It had been a long time since Steve had been to the hotel, and he gasped as he stood in the lobby. It was like entering a palace—an oasis from the cold, dirty streets he had grown accustomed to. The white marble floors gleamed, a huge chandelier glowed warmly and accents of gold glittered everywhere. The lobby ceiling did not stop at the main floor, but extended beyond to the second floor. The sheer stature of the lobby could have been imposing, but only served as an inviting entrance to the grand hotel.

"Excuse me."

Steve realized that while he stood in awe of his surroundings, he was also blocking others who were trying to exit through the revolving doors. He moved quickly out of the way, and that was when he noticed Penny way ahead of him already. She was smiling at him and waving frantically for him to hurry. She was wearing her long, black down-filled coat, warm winter boots and a baby blue wool tam. She looked ridiculous, and just the sight of her caused Steve to make a bold decision: the wedding would take place here.

Penny was heading straight to the front desk. She had done her research and was hoping to secure a tour of Room 202, the one said to be haunted by a woman in a cloak. Some claimed they saw the walls bleed and heard the window shatter. The Winnipeg Free Press had even reported that a Liberal MP from Ontario stayed in the room and said spirits trying to share her bed awakened her! The politician had ended up in the lobby, in her housecoat, completely terrified. They had to move her to another room.

Penny was skeptical about her resolve to go through with the tour, if they'd even give her one, but figured she could do it with Steve beside her. She had to try.

Penny had developed a fascination with local ghosts and their histories. It had started with the ghost of Edith at the Marlborough Hotel and now had brought her to the Hotel Fort Garry. Her fascination is what had driven her to writing. She had a strong urge to tell their stories, and maybe, in some odd way, bring them some peace.

Steve headed toward her and could tell she wasn't having much luck persuading the front desk clerk for a tour. As Penny continued to talk, he was shaking his head and attempting to move on with his duties, until Steve arrived by her side, and stood his full height.

"Is it available to tour now dear, or should we have lunch first?"

The front desk clerk quit his charade of shuffling papers and gave Steve his full attention. "I'm sorry sir, I'm sure you'll understand. We just don't have time for ghost tours."

"Ghost tours? What are you talking about? We are looking at booking our wedding. What is your biggest ballroom?"

Penny gave Steve a nudge and stifled a giggle as the front desk clerk became nervous.

"Oh, just a moment, I'll get Naomi down to see you immediately."

A few minutes later, Naomi expertly descended the staircase in very high heels, while still managing to fumble her arms into her suit jacket. She introduced herself and shook both Steve and Penny's hands, and extended congratulations on their engagement. She looked suspiciously at Penny's bare left ring finger.

"Where shall we start? The ballroom?"

"Actually, and most importantly, we'd like to see our honeymoon suite." Steve winked at Naomi as he said it. He was sure he heard Penny groan.

Naomi smiled knowingly, "Of course, we have the most romantic honeymoon suite." She outstretched an arm that led them to the elevator.

"I'm sure you do, Naomi, but you see my fiancée is a writer. She's writing a ghost story about the hotel, and really has her heart set on spending the night in Room 202."

"Oh? Anything I might have read?"

"Not yet!" Penny piped.

The elevator was small, and Penny was starting to have regrets about the whole thing. When the doors opened Naomi and Steve exited quickly. Penny only followed so not to be left alone. Naomi chirped about the especially wide hallways and how they were specifically designed this way, back in the day, to accommodate the ladies' wide-skirted dresses. They arrived at the door to Room 202 much too soon for Penny. Just the sight of the closed door gave her the chills. The hallway was silent, and the click of the card lock opening the door resounded in Penny's head. Naomi had to insert it several times before the green light finally lit up, securing their fate, in Penny's mind.

The three of them stood in the room together. It was small and so very quiet. Other than the eerie silence in the room, it seemed perfectly normal. Penny's fear had remarkably vanished once they were inside; she even found the room quite charming. Steve wasn't as comfortable, and wandered about the room to veil his unease. It was not the haunted room that had him spooked. He looked out the window and commented on the snow coming down. Penny noticed he was tapping his thigh again and wondered why. Not only was he tapping he wouldn't stand still. He opened drawers and then closed them. He opened the closet, and then shut it very quickly.

Naomi's cellphone dinged and she motioned with her finger that she'd just be a minute, and then she left them alone in the room. Penny looked hard at Steve.

"What's got into you?" she asked.

"So? You want to have our wedding here, Pen?"

"Oh Steve, you can quit the charade. We're alone now, and we got to see the room. I didn't know what a conniver you were, but thanks."

Penny pulled a camera out of her bag and began taking pictures.

"I mean it Penny. I thought you did too. You said yes at the hospital!"

She stopped dead. Turning to look at Steve she could see he was shaking. He remembered his proposal, and he had meant it!

Their conversation was disrupted by an insistent knocking on the door.

"I can't seem to open the door, can you please open it." It was Naomi on the other side. Penny and Steve paid her no mind. They just stood there staring at each other. Finally Steve spoke.

"Do I have to ask you again? Penny, will you marry me?"

A loud crack of breaking glass resounded in the room. They both looked at the window. One of the panes had shattered. A strong wind blew in swirling snowflakes. The closet door flew open and slammed shut again. An icy chill passed through them both.

Penny flew herself at Steve, wrapped her legs around his waist and her arms around his neck. With her face buried in his shoulder she screamed, "No-o-o-o-o!"

CHAPTER FOURTEEN

"So let me get this straight. First she said yes, then no, then yes again. I don't know, Steve. I'm not all that confident spending my hard-earned cash on dry-cleaning my old suit when the bride is so unsure."

Randall smirked and leaned back on the couch, folding his arms over his chest. His dark brown hair was parted in the middle and tied back into a long braid. He wore a dark blue Levi denim shirt. He was in good shape, and even with the shirt tucked into his jeans there was no excess at his midriff. He stood barely taller than five feet, but with his strength and sturdiness he looked taller. Big brown eyes resided behind oversized black-rimmed glasses. The man was in his mid-30s, but there were no wrinkles in that face. A small scar on his chin only added to his character.

Everyone laughed at Randall's ribbing, everyone but Steve, who only rolled his eyes and was thankful he wasn't sitting close, or he would have surely suffered one of Randall's jabs to his ribs.

Miraculously, the wedding was set for Friday, February 14 at the Hotel Fort Garry. Penny and Steve had invited Steve's partner Grant, and his wife, Angel, over to celebrate. They also invited their good friend Randall and his wife, Rose. Randall loved to tease Steve, but Rose usually chided him for it.

His wife possessed a quiet beauty. Even when she scolded Randall, Rose smiled. Her smile was warm and it transformed her whole face. Her cheeks would plump up and cause her eyes to squint adoringly. To Randall's relief, she was shorter than him. Over the years, with each child, she had put on some weight. Randall didn't mind, and always told her it was just more to love. She carried her weight well and never hid it under baggy clothes. Tonight she wore a deep purple fitted tee with form-fitting jeans. A pendant locket always hung around her neck. Her dark hair, with its natural waves, fell freely just to her shoulders.

Penny held onto Steve's arm with both her hands. "No worries, Randall, dry clean away. I'm not letting this guy get away."

"Yes, Randall, you can get your suit cleaned, invest in a new tie, and hey, maybe consider a haircut." Steve regretted his words instantly. Rose reached for Randall's long braid. Eyes downcast, she held it with one hand and smoothed it lovingly with the other. Penny let go of Steve's arm and gave him the look.

Randall only laughed, got up and poked Steve in the ribs. "Good one."

Steve let out a sigh of relief, shrugged his shoulders and gave Penny a sheepish look.

Penny had worked with Randall at the Marlborough for many years, and Steve and Randall had become good friends during the time Steve worked there. Rose was a dear, and the four of them were normally cozy company.

Tonight was a bit strained. It was the first time Steve and Penny had met Grant's wife, Angel. When Grant and Angel first arrived, Steve took one look at Angel and had to agree with Grant. She did have the face of an angel. He sensed her to be a somewhat distressed angel, but a very attractive one just the same. She had the most beautiful blond hair.

"So Angel, Grant tells me you're thinking of starting your own business." Steve said.

"Yes."

He continued. "What kind of business are you opening?"

"I don't know."

Angel did not elaborate, and the conversation was at a standstill.

"Dinner's ready!" yelled Penny from the kitchen just in time.

It always surprised Steve what a good cook Penny was. It just didn't fit somehow, but he was glad. She wasn't an adventurous cook, but she could sure mix a fresh salad and grill a good steak. Tonight she went all out and made her stuffed baked potatoes.

Once everyone was seated and food was being passed, the dinner table became lively. Everyone chattered above each other. The only quiet one was Angel, and Penny thought she understood why. Everyone else knew each other so well. It was the first time Angel had met any of them. Penny attempted to draw her into the conversation. When she asked her for advice on being married to a detective that finally got her talking, and she had a lot to say.

"I sure hope you know what you're getting into, Penny."

"Why do you say that?"

The others chattered on while Penny and Angel carried on their own conversation.

"It's the waiting and the worry I find the worst."

"Well, I'm afraid I know a bit about that already, but I keep busy with my writing. It makes the time go by quick."

"You're lucky, then. I have nothing. Since I quit my job I just stumble around the house and worry the whole time Grant's at work. Then when it's almost time for his shift to end, I park myself in the front window and watch for him. God forbid he's ever late."

"Sounds like you might need something to occupy your time Angel. Steve tells me you're starting your own business."

"Oh that. Yes. Well, some day. You know when I'm waiting for him, I imagine so many terrible things. Sometimes I get myself in such a state."

Angel took a sip of wine and gave Penny a small smile.

"Well, I can understand. When I got the call when Steve got hurt, I was a real mess."

"That's another thing: every time the phone rings I jump, then I'm afraid to even answer it."

Penny found the conversation making her uncomfortable and went quiet. This gave Angel a chance to share her horror stories of police stats of injuries, or even loss of life on the job. Penny could take no more. She smiled and got up to clear some plates and offered, "Well, thank goodness for cellphones, at least we can track them down if we have to."

Angel called to Penny as she walked to the kitchen. "Yes, cellphones are great—when they answer. I don't know how many times I've called Grant and been sent to voicemail."

"Aha! So you're the one who calls Grant every five minutes." Steve laughed and took another big sip of his wine.

Angel's face went pale. Grant glared at Steve. All conversation was halted, and all eyes were on Steve.

Penny stood at the kitchen doorway and sighed. "You'll have to excuse my fiancé. He can be a bit of an ass at times, and obviously can't hold his liquor."

This time everyone laughed, and Randall raised his glass for a toast. "I'll drink to that."

Steve gave Penny a sideways glance. They both knew it was she who couldn't hold her liquor. Still, what she said got him out of an awkward spot.

Randall stood. "Here's to the lovely couple. Steve, if she must find you to be an ass, at least let it be a nice piece of ass."

Rose slapped Randall's shoulder with the back of her hand, but she smiled and lifted her glass with everyone else.

Later, over coffee and dessert, the raucous group had subdued somewhat. As they sat comfortably on Steve's large sectional, the conversation turned to the wedding plans.

"You mean you're really going to stay in that room for your wedding night, after what happened?" Rose's eyes bulged.

"It was just a little wind," Steve said. "And the cold made the glass brittle. It could happen anywhere."

"What he's really trying to say is he can't wait to marry me and the hotel is busy, so we didn't have a lot of choices."

"What she'd trying to say is she's not scared of anything when I'm around." Steve puffed up his chest and Randall, who sat beside him, took the opportunity to poke him again.

Steve wailed, "Someone please change seats with me!"

Surprising everyone, Angel got up and squeezed between the two of them. Penny felt a small surge of jealousy rising, but knew enough to let it go.

"More coffee anyone?"

Grant stood up, "No thanks Penny, Angel and I better get going."

After they left, Rose asked Penny how her book was coming along. Penny jumped at the chance to discuss it and ran and got her laptop. Snuggled on the couch together Penny explained how, scared as she was, she wanted to spend the night in Room 202 at the Hotel Fort Garry.

"I'll be fine. Steve promised to never leave me in there alone. Plus, I'm trying to face some of my fears to get over them."

"Really? Why?"

"Well, I spoke to a young man once. He told me how he was claustrophobic and scared of heights. So what does he do? He takes a job giving cave tours and running a zip-line."

"Did that help him?"

"Sure did, so I figure if I'm going to write about ghosts, I better get over my fear of them. Now the ghost at the Hotel Fort Garry is said to..."

Rose leaned in to listen.

Randall grabbed a couple of the dessert plates off the coffee table and headed to the kitchen. He motioned with a neck tilt for Steve to follow.

When Steve walked in, Randall was already filling the sink. Steve went to the fridge and grabbed a couple of beers. He held one out for Randall. "We have a dishwasher."

"Oh. Good." Randall turned off the water and opened his beer.

It was a small galley kitchen, separate from the dining area. Both men leaned against a counter opposite of each other, and enjoyed their beer.

"I had to get away from their spook talk." Randal shivered dramatically.

"Actually I wanted to ask you something. I was, uh, wondering if you'd be my best man."

Randall set his beer down on the counter. He looked at Steve a moment and then said, "Sure, I can do that."

"Great."

Randall picked up his beer and conversation moved on.

"Still scared of ghosts, aren't you."

Randall said nothing, but only gave him a look and shook his finger warningly at him.

CHAPTER FIFTEEN

Steve leaned back in his chair and threw a paper clip into an old Styrofoam coffee cup. It went in. He had only missed a few so far.

His desk phone began to ring and he quickly sat up on his chair and answered.

"Detective Steve Ascot."

"Hey Steve, it's Grant."

"You coming in?"

"Yeah, just wanted to let you know I'll be in a little late."

"OK, see you when you get here."

Steve picked up a pen and grabbed a file folder out of his drawer. He was going to wait for Grant before he got started on the paperwork, but figured he may as well do it now. Grant could look it over when he got in. Leaning back in his chair he opened the folder, took in a deep breath and released it with a groan. Most detectives hated this part of the job, and Steve wasn't much different. Still, he knew the importance of this part of the job and always prided himself on his precision reports.

So absorbed in his work, he was able to block out the chatter in the office. It was only when one of the younger detectives slapped him on the back that he looked up.

"Good job on the case Steve, wrapped it up nice and tidy."

Steve looked up at him. "Thanks, Buddy."

The guys name was actually Buddy. Steve had run-ins with him before, wasn't too impressed with the guy, but reserved judgment until he could get to know him a bit better.

"Too bad about the leg, though. You have to watch out for those little kids. They're tough these days."

Buddy laughed and Steve heard someone else snicker. Steve decided then that he really didn't like this guy. He stood to his full height and looked him in the eye. Just as he was about to put this guy in his place, Penny walked in.

"Hi. Hope you don't mind me stopping by." She held up a brown bag. "You left this in the fridge."

Steve smiled. Penny had obviously gone to a bit of effort to look extra nice before she stopped in. She had more than succeeded in the green angora sweater he had bought her for Christmas. It was almost a little snug, but Steve thought it looked great. The whole office had gone quiet, and they all looked her way. She smiled nervously as she looked around the place. Steve pulled out a chair for her and gave everyone a mind-your-own-business glare, and they did.

"Where's Grant?" She pointed to his nameplate on the empty desk across from Steve.

"Oh, he called, going to be a bit late. Want to grab a coffee?"

"Sure, but not from here, right?"

Steve smiled. She had been here before, and he knew how much she hated their coffee.

"No, let's go across the street."

Penny was sure she heard a whistle as they walked out, but she stared straight ahead. Steve looked back, though, and she imagined he gave them an icy glare.

When Steve returned from coffee with Penny, Grant was already at his desk. He was just grabbing for the folder off Steve's desk to get started on the paperwork.

Steve quickly took off his coat and hung it on the rack. He grabbed the folder from Grant and said, "That's OK, I've filled out hundreds of these. Besides, I already got started on it. I don't mind."

Grant yanked the folder back and slammed it on his desk. "What the hell Steve, you don't think I can fill out some damn paperwork?"

Steve backed away. "Whoa, what's with you?"

Grant glared at Steve. "Fuck all, that's all!"

Steve held up both hands, palms facing forward. "OK, OK, just asking." Grant sure wasn't acting like he was OK, but Steve could tell the guy needed some breathing room, so he went and sat at his own desk. He left the folder with Grant.

The two of them worked quietly for some time, barely looking up at each other. Grant stared at the papers in the folder, but Steve could tell he wasn't really seeing them. He never even turned the page. Finally Grant broke the silence with a small gesture of apology, without actually making one.

"You want to go grab some lunch?"

Steve discreetly dropped his brown bag lunch in the trash can under his desk. "Sure, I'm starving."

Steve drove. They would have normally headed out for a quick burger, but Steve had the feeling Grant needed to talk. He drove to Rae and Jerry's Steakhouse. They served a good steak sandwich, and the place wasn't noisy; they'd be able to talk. It took a few minutes to get there, and the whole time Grant never said a word, but only stared out the window.

Once inside and seated, Grant stared blankly at the menu. Their waitress was cheerful and polite, but even she could sense the cloud looming over Grant's head. She brought everything they needed, but never hung around. Steve chatted as much as he could and would ask Grant the odd question or his opinion. Grant only ate half of his lunch and spent most of the time staring into his plate. When they had finished Steve couldn't take it anymore.

"OK, Grant, what the hell's going on?"

Grant looked at Steve and then down at the table. "I hit her."

"What? Who?"

"Angel. I slapped her right across the face."

Steve sat back in his chair and placed both hands on the table and let out a long, slow, deep breath. Neither of them spoke for minutes.

"I don't know how I could hit her. She's so damn beautiful. I slapped that beautiful face!"

Steve couldn't believe what he was hearing. He knew Grant had a temper, but Grant wasn't the kind of guy that would hit his wife, or any woman for that matter.

"I just lost it Steve, I was so fucking mad!"

Steve watched Grant as he stared down while he twisted his cloth napkin with both hands.

The waitress brought their bill and placed it on the table. She was smiling and began to say something, but one look at the two of them and she turned on her heals and headed the other way.

"Take it easy Grant, just tell me what happened."

"I was going crazy all night. She wouldn't answer her phone; I had no idea where she was. I was worried as hell. I was even going to call you, Steve."

"You should have."

"I paced the house, I kept calling her. I even went for a drive to look for her car, but once I was on the road I realized I had no idea where to look. She'd been pretty down since she left her job. I thought the worst."

"But she finally came home, and—"

"Yeah, at 3:30 am! Where does a person go till that time of night? I was sitting on the couch in the dark when I saw her car headlights pull into the driveway. I just sat there, Steve. Then I heard her key open the door and she came in all quiet. She took off her shoes at the door and headed for the stairs. She nearly jumped out of her skin when I called her name."

"So where was she?"

"Who knows, she wouldn't say. She was all nervous and then made up some story about having coffee with a friend. That was bullshit! She never has coffee with a friend, Steve."

Grant threw his napkin on the table. Steve could see that the more he talked about it, the more agitated he became.

"Calm down Grant, you need to take it—"

"I told her I was worried sick about her all night. I demanded she tell me where she really was, why she didn't answer her damn phone. Instead of giving me an explanation she said nothing, and then she just turned and walked away from me."

Grant's hands were shaking now. He held them up and stared at them. "I ran after her, Steve, grabbed her by the shoulders and spun her around to face me, and you know what she did? She fuckin' laughed."

"Is that when you, well, you know…"

"I don't know what came over me. I wound up and I slapped her square in the face. Hard, Steve, I hit her hard!"

Grant dropped his forehead into both his hands. Steve could see their waitress behind the bar, pretending not to watch them. Then, for the first time, Grant looked straight at Steve, right into his eyes. "I hit her hard, and you know what, she didn't cry, or yell, or anything. She just took one long look at me and went upstairs to bed."

"Then what did you do?" Steve hoped nothing more.

"God, Steve! I slept on the couch, and when I got up she was in the kitchen making coffee, as if nothing had happened. Except when I looked at her, that angel face, it had a big fucking bruise on it and one of her fucking eyes was swollen."

"I'm really sorry Grant, you must feel like shit. Did you manage to talk things out?"

"Nope, she wouldn't say one word to me."

They sat in silence for a few minutes. Steve didn't know what to say, so he picked up their bill and went to the bar to pay. When he got back to the table Grant was more composed. Steve figured just telling him what happened had helped somewhat.

"Sorry to lay all this on you Steve, what do I owe you?"

"My treat. Let's go."

The drive back was quiet again and once back at the office they didn't talk any more about it, but Steve was worried. In their line of work, personal problems could be a dangerous distraction. He wondered if he should talk to Chief Dan, but decided that breaking Grant's confidence wouldn't help their working relationship. He decided he'd just wait to see how things went.

There was no denying he was shocked that Grant had hit his pretty wife, but he was sure it was totally out of character. Grant was no wife-beater. Something wasn't right.

Their desks faced each other and Steve fidgeted uncomfortably in his. He couldn't mention anything about their lunch discussion and at the same time he couldn't make light conversation either. So they worked in silence. When Grant's phone rang, Steve jumped. He hoped it was Angel. They really needed to talk this thing out, not pretend it never happened.

"Grant Mayne here. What? No, Christ, I paid that last month." Grant got up from his desk and headed to the hallway to finish the call.

Steve was sorry to even hear part of that call and was disappointed for Grant that it wasn't Angel. When Grant and Steve started working together she used to call him constantly; now, it was barely ever. Obviously something had changed.

Steve wished he knew the whole story. He wanted to help them. He suspected she was up to no good, but he knew Grant loved her a lot, and he could tell she was seriously troubled; he saw it in her eyes the evening she was over for dinner.

On one hand he wanted to mind his own business. On the other, with Grant as his partner, it really was his business. Besides, despite Grant's temper flare-ups he was really starting to like the guy. He made a decision. He would find out what was going on, where Angel was spending all her time and where all their money was going.

Then, just maybe he could figure out a way to help.

CHAPTER SIXTEEN

Penny was amazed how excited she was for their wedding. She was still uncertain how she felt about the whole institution of marriage, after the dismal failure of her first, but with Steve it all felt different; it felt new and very real. And after that kid knifed him, when she didn't know how bad it was, or whether he would even make it, she realized how much she needed him in her life. She knew then that life without him would be no life at all.

He was full of surprises. The man she'd pegged as a confirmed bachelor wanted to get married. She had fully expected they would have a small wedding. Her first wedding had been huge, and that was enough for her. Steve had surprised her again. He wanted to go all out with a full wedding. He had laughed and teased her, said it was his first and her last, so he wanted it to be memorable.

So now, here she was in a bridal shop, picking out another wedding dress. She had decided to come alone, to not be influenced by anyone else's opinion. The dress had to be perfect. Now that she was in the shop she had lost her bravado and wished she had brought her Mom or even Steve. She stared at the never-ending rows of wall-to-wall poof, lace and crinolines. How would she ever find that ideal dress amongst so many! Just as she was going to give up and head for the door, a tall and elegant young woman gently approached her.

"Are you looking for a wedding dress?"

"Yes, how did you know? Oh of course…" Penny blushed at her stupidity. There she was in a bridal shop with a shiny engagement ring on her finger.

"Let me guess, you want something beautiful, elegant and flattering. Not too much poof. Am I right?"

Penny's face relaxed and she smiled, "Yes, that's it exactly—and, of course, it has to be perfect."

"Of course it does, and you know, I think I might have just the one. It came in today, and I knew the minute you walked in it was sent for you. I've been admiring it all morning."

Penny thought, yeah right, that easy.

The sales girl disappeared in the back and Penny had to sit down. She was feeling a bit overwhelmed. There was a chair by the change rooms, button-tuft ivory, and it sat to the side on a huge, round elevated floor, like a stage. Surrounding the stage were walls of mirrors to the ceiling. Looking into the mirror, a cavalcade of her reflections looked back. She looked away, down at her shoes, but a ruffling noise and a sudden flitter of motion brought her attention back to the mirrors. She was surprised to see another bride-to-be's reflections scurrying behind her. She hadn't noticed anyone else in the store when she arrived. The woman had blond curls, but Penny could not see her face, for with her wedding dress she also had the most beautiful hooded cloak. Before Penny could catch her attention to say hello, she disappeared into a change room.

The saleslady returned, carefully carrying a dress bag draped over both her extended arms. With a pleasant smile she motioned for Penny to follow. She hung the dress on the outside hook of a dressing room door. Penny was sure it was the same room claimed by the other bride-to-be.

"Oh, I think that one is occupied."

"Occupied? No, it's just you here today." She flung open the door and she was right, it was empty.

"No, there was a blond woman trying on a wedding dress…"

The saleslady simply tilted her head, looked at Penny and smiled warmly.

Penny was puzzled, but decided it best to say no more. She entered the large dressing room. More mirrors. The saleslady entered as well and hung the dress inside and removed the plastic covering.

"Will you need any help?"

"No, thank you, I'll be fine."

The door clicked shut and before Penny even looked at the dress, she knelt down and looked under the spaces of the dressing room walls. Had she been mistaken which room the other bride had gone into? Nope, nothing, there were no feet on either side. I must have imagined it, she thought.

As she stood up her eyes fell upon the most beautiful dress she could have ever imagined. She forgot all about the other bride and quickly removed her jeans and T-shirt. Her only hope was that she could do the dress justice. She removed it from the hanger and carefully stepped into it. The long satin skirt fell loosely, and the bodice draped in a sweetheart neckline.

"How's it going?"

"Oh good, but I guess I will need some help with the zipper."

Penny stepped out. The salesgirl carefully pulled up the zipper, and then motioned with an outstretched arm for Penny to step up onto the round stage.

Penny took one look, and before she even knew the price, said, "I'll take it."

Steve fidgeted while the man, who Steve figured had to be at least 150 years old, measured his inseam. In truth he was probably only about 90. Steve knew the guy was the best tailor in the city, but also knew now he was the slowest-moving person in the world.

"Stand still!!"

Steve concentrated hard on not moving. Only his gaze darted around the shop. He decided it probably looked no different than the day it opened, which would have been a very long time ago. He knew the shop was opened originally by the old man's father.

Except for the odd red bow tie or such, the place was practically colourless, resembling an old faded photo. Large spools of thread reached as high as the ceiling and racks of jackets on wooden hangers covered the back wall. A murky front window displayed a dusty jacket, tie and shirt ensemble on a half mannequin with no head.

The old guy was thin with balding, grey hair, and wore heavy, dark-rimmed glasses. His pants were beige and were held up with clipped-on suspenders over a crisp white shirt. Steve was impressed with how limber the man was as he twisted and turned to measure this way and that. Before they could quite finish the measurements, Steve cringed as he heard his phone ring. It was in his jacket pocket hanging on a wooden chair across the room.

"Sorry, I have to get that."

With a mouthful of straight pins pursed between his lips, the tailor stood with hands on hips and stared a moment, then he rolled his eyes and threw his tape measure dramatically over his shoulder and shuffled slowly over to his machine and sat down.

"Detective Steve Ascot."

The tailor looked up and pushed his glasses down his nose. He looked over at Steve and raised an eyebrow.

"It's just me, I found it!"

"Penny? What did you find?"

"My wedding dress, of course. Are we still meeting for lunch?"

Steve had other plans. He had forgotten about meeting Penny for lunch.

"You didn't forget, did you?"

"Uh, no, of course not, I was, uh, just thinking about Angel and …"

"Angel! Grant's wife! Why were you thinking about her?"

"Penny, please, I'll explain later. Can you pick me up?"

"OK, you still at the tailor?"

"Yes, I have the car, but if you still have your parents' I'd prefer to take that."

"You're kidding. I thought you hated riding in the rusted red pony? It's so small your head hits the roof."

"Just come and get me."

Steve shoved the phone back in his jacket pocket.

The tailor was already in position with his tape measure. He had pulled over a wooden crate and stood on it to measure Steve's shoulder and neck. Eye-to-eye now, he looked at Steve and smiled. "Big case, detective?"

Just as they were finishing they heard a car horn honking outside the shop. Through the murky window, Steve could see Penny smiling and waving from inside the car. He felt good; she had that effect on him. He quickly thanked the tailor and dashed out the door as he put on his jacket. The bell on the door jingled as he left.

"It's in the back seat!"

Steve was trying to manouevre his tall frame into the small car, and as he pushed his seat back she screamed.

"What?"

"My dress! It's in the back seat—be careful you don't crush it."

Penny was now almost halfway in the back seat to make sure it was OK. From where he sat, her rear end and the back of her legs were all he could see of her.

"Is it OK?"

"Yeah, it's good, I just—"

Steve grabbed her by the waist and pulled her over to him. He wrapped his strong arms around her delicate frame and held her tight. She looked up at him, tilted her head and smiled. He smiled too and then he kissed her.

Penny felt the kiss throughout her whole being. She had to pull herself away, back into her own seat.

She looked at him sideways. "Miss me?"

"You could tell?"

Penny put on her seatbelt and put the car in gear. "Where to?"

"I'm looking for an Angel."

"You better hope it's an angel of mercy!"

CHAPTER SEVENTEEN

Penny had been so excited to tell Steve all about her dress that she pretty much dismissed his comment on looking for an angel. He told her he didn't have much time and needed her to drive him somewhere, and asked if she minded just going to a fast food drive-through. She was still telling him about trying on the dress and never even answered him, but when he pointed, she pulled in quickly to the drive-through and asked, "What do you want?"

"Get me a Papa Burger, onion rings and a root beer."

Penny was pretty hungry herself so she ordered herself the same, except she chose fries instead of onion rings.

"Somebody better watch what they eat if they want to fit that dress in the back seat!"

"Somebody better shut up unless they want—"

"Will that be cash or debit?"

"Cash," said Steve as he reached his arm past Penny and paid. "Keep the change."

Penny was going to pull into a spot in the parking lot to eat, but Steve told her to keep going and drive west on Portage Avenue.

"Where are we going? I'm hungry, and I can't eat and drive."

"It's not far, just a few blocks down."

"Remind me to never make a lunch date with you again. And why do you need to find Angel anyway?"

"It's a long story, Penny. Let's just get there, park, and I'll tell you everything while we eat."

Penny's eyes gleamed. "Are we on a stakeout?"

"Well if it makes you happy to call it that, and you promise to have lunch with me in the future, sure, we can call it a stakeout."

Penny grabbed a pair of her dad's old sunglasses off the visor, flipped up the collar on her jacket and dramatically raised her eyebrows up and down at Steve.

Steve laughed and shook his head. "Oh Lord, what have I done."

Once they arrived at Grant's house, Steve instructed Penny to park on the opposite side of the street, a few doors down. The street was wide, allowing for parking on both sides. Most of the homes were old two-stories with small front yards. Some were fairly well kept, while others were in obvious need of repair. Grant and Angel's home was somewhere in between. It looked like it could use a fresh coat of paint, and a loose shutter on the front window looked ready to fall. A plastic Christmas angel on the front step had fallen over and had gathered a layer of snow.

While they ate, Steve told Penny all about his concerns. He told her how Angel used to call Grant about every hour, on the hour, and now the calls had stopped. How he suspected they were having money problems, yet even on only Grant's salary, they should be doing OK. Then he told her Grant couldn't find Angel the night before and how she had tried to sneak in at 3:30 am. He purposely left out the part about Grant hitting her. He wasn't sure why he didn't tell her; it just felt wrong.

"Well that doesn't sound good Steve, but I'm surprised at you, wanting to spy on Angel."

"I know, I don't like it either, but I like the guy, I want to help him out. See if I can find out what Angel is up to." Steve didn't want to explain to Penny how important it is to everyone's safety that your partner is focused on the job. He didn't want to worry her.

"There she is!"

Angel was getting into her car. She too wore dark glasses, but Steve knew the real reason for them.

"OK, just drive normally Penny, but stay a few car lengths behind. It's better to lose her than have her figure out she's being followed."

It wasn't that hard to follow Angel. She simply headed west on Portage Avenue and drove until she was just out of the city. She pulled into an out-of-the-way bar in the first small town she came to. She manoeuvred her car with confidence, like she had been there before. The parking lot was almost empty, yet she chose a parking spot at the far end. Penny and Steve watched from the gas station across the street.

"Why the heck would she go to a bar way out here in the middle of the day?"

"I don't know Pen, but I doubt it's for the ambience."

"Now what? Do we go in or wait?"

"Neither; we head back. This was a good start, but Grant will be wondering what's taking me so long."

The drive back was quiet. Penny was no longer excited about having been part of a stakeout. It was all just too sad that Grant and Angel were having trouble. Steve was very quiet, and Penny held back from interrupting his thoughts as long as she could.

"You OK?"

"Yeah, I'm fine."

"What do you think she was doing there, Steve?"

"I don't know, Pen, most people go to a bar to drink, but I don't think that's it."

"Oh for sure not, who would drive out of the city to drink when you can sit at home and drink all you want in your own home."

"You're scaring me Pen. Is that what I have to look forward to?"

"Be serious. I mean really, this is bothering me. But I'm pretty sure we can rule out drinking. She barely finished her first glass of wine at our place that night they were over."

"True."

They were both quiet with their own thoughts again until Penny blurted, "Oh my God, you don't think she's stripping for extra money, do you? You said they had money troubles!"

Steve laughed at Penny's alarm. "No, I don't think that's it. Angel's not the type, too classy, but she does have the body for it."

Steve regretted the words even as he said them. He always spoke his mind to her; he forgot sometimes how fragile she could be. Penny hit the brakes, stopped right in the middle of the road. "Oh, so you've checked that out, have you?"

"Not in the way you're thinking, Penny. If you haven't noticed, I happen to be crazy about you, and only you."

Penny did not reply; she just stared straight ahead.

"Aw come on Pen, don't do that."

Again, she didn't reply. Steve rested his hand gently on her shoulder and that seemed to work. At least she spoke

"Don't do what."

"You know, get all jealous and mad for no reason."

"Well I think I have very good reason when you tell me how great a body another woman has!"

"You're right, I'm an oaf, but please don't be mad. I shouldn't have said it. I'm not the most sensitive guy. I'm always honest with you and feel I can say anything to you, but maybe I should be more careful."

Penny reached her hand and slapped his shoulder. "Oh forget it. You can tell me anything, Steve. Sorry, guess I overreact at times. But you're right."

"I am?"

"Yeah, you are an oaf."

There wasn't much traffic mid-afternoon, but still a few cars still had to drive around them, and a few honked.

"OK Pen, yes I am, but could you please drive now."

Penny could tell Steve was still upset, not with her, but with the whole Angel and Grant thing. She could always tell when he was worried; he would repeatedly tap his hand on his thigh. She reached over and held his hand until it was still.

"Steve? You think she's playing the VLTs? It might explain their money problems. My mom had a friend who got really hooked on playing them. It got pretty bad. They ended up losing their home."

"Yes that would explain a lot, their money problems, plus people with a gambling addiction like to go to an out-of-the-way place to play, especially a detective's wife. Good work Pen. But it doesn't explain where she was till 3:30 in the morning."

"No. Do you think she's meeting someone?"

"I sure hope not. I don't know if Grant could handle that. He really loves her, you know."

They rode the rest of the way in silence, each quiet in their own thoughts.

Penny dropped Steve back at the tailors to get his car and he headed straight back to work. When he pulled into the parking lot at headquarters, Grant was just coming out the door.

"Where you been, Steve? We just got a call. Someone found us a cold one while out walking their dog."

Both of them headed head back to the car, put the light on the roof, and sped off. When they arrived at the scene, there were already a few patrol cars, and police cruisers blocked off the area. Police were also putting up crime-scene tape.

Steve was on alert. He walked slowly, compiling a mental picture of the scene to memory, taking in every minute detail. It often served as a valuable reference. The victim was a guy. He looked fairly young, but it was hard to tell. It looked like he'd been out in the cold for a while. The cause of death was pretty obvious—a bullet entry wound right in the middle of his forehead.

"Has forensics been notified?" he asked a few of the patrols.

"Yes sir, on their way."

"Better start canvassing the homes in the area, see if anybody knows anything."

"Already started."

"Good."

It was another bitterly cold January day in Winnipeg, and Steve knew they'd be out there a while. He grabbed his toque out of his pocket and pulled it on his head.

"What do you think, Steve?"

"Too soon to make any assumptions Grant, the evidence will tell us all we need to know." This was the most crucial point of any investigation. He was on his way to instruct the officers putting up the crime scene tape to expand the area. He pulled out his note pad and was just about to jot a few things down when Grant caught up with him.

"Hey Steve, you know I'm sorry about laying all my marital problems on you, you know, especially with your own wedding just a couple weeks away."

Steve didn't want to discuss this now, when they were in the middle of an investigation that needed his full attention. "Yeah, yeah, Grant no worries. Can we talk about this later?"

"Oh sure Steve, I just wanted to let you know how bad I feel about dragging you into my drama."

Steve was barely listening, "Like I said; no worries."

"You know she's not answering her phone again. I wish the hell I knew where she went all the time. It's starting to really get to me."

Now Steve was paying attention. He could tell Grant wanted to pursue the conversation. He didn't, mainly because he had to focus, but also because he had a big pang of guilt. He knew where Angel was, but he couldn't tell Grant without admitting to following her. No, he had to keep quiet until he knew more.

"Yeah, I get why you're worried…" Steve noticed a cigarette butt on the ground and pulled out a small plastic bag and gloves. "Really though, Grant, we can talk later. Let's see if we can't help figure out what happened to this poor guy first."

Grant walked away without another word.

CHAPTER EIGHTEEN

After she had dropped Steve off at his car Penny had planned on heading straight over to her parents' to show them her dress. It still needed a few alterations, but she just had to take it with her when she had left the store. When Steve had tried to maneuver his large frame from her parents' small car, he knocked his knee against the glove compartment, it flew open and several wedding invitations had flittered out.

He had fumbled to pick them up and asked why she hadn't delivered them!

She had grabbed the stack from his hands and blushing told him, "Of course I did. I mailed most of them. These are just a few for the Marlborough." She had stuffed them in her large purse and assured him that she had spoken to them all on the phone already, and explained that she had just never got around to dropping them off.

So now, instead of heading to her parents, she was heading to the Marlborough. It was a cold day and the roads were slippery. Traffic was quite heavy and the exhaust from the other cars emitted large clouds of fog, hampering visibility. When she finally reached the front entrance of the Marlborough she was relieved to see a parking spot right out front. She was tempted to leave the car running so it would stay warm, but knew it was out of the question. With her wedding dress in the back seat, she knew she had to lock it up before going in.

A biting cold wind practically blew her through the front door. Standing inside the lobby, Penny realized she had never actually come back to the hotel since she had left her job at the front desk. It all looked the same, yet felt strangely foreign.

Randall had already spotted her. "Penny! Wait, don't tell me. Steve finally came to his senses and decided not to give up his bachelor life. I suppose you're here to beg for your job back."

Penny just smiled and headed to the front desk. She really missed working with Randall, even if he was a smart aleck.

"Hardly. I'm just here to drop off your wedding invite." She slapped the stack on the front desk counter.

"Well it's about time. I've been checking the mail for weeks." Randall faked a forlorn look.

"Oh stop it. There's a few more there that I hope you'll give out."

"So other than inviting your guests, how's the wedding plans coming along?"

"Not bad, I found my dress today."

As they chatted a lady from housekeeping arrived at the front desk. She just stood quietly, obviously needing to speak to Randall, but not wanting to interrupt.

"A little last minute," he said, "but one would expect no less from you. How's the writing coming along?"

"Good. And I'm actually really excited to stay in the haunted room at the Hotel Fort Garry."

The lady from housekeeping pressed a hand to her chest and gasped. Randall and Penny both stopped their conversation and looked at her.

"You OK Bonny?"

"Yes, I just, did you say Miss that you are staying in the haunted room?"

"I did, Room 202."

"Mercy no. You mustn't."

"Oh I must, you see I'm a writer, or trying to be, and I'm writing about local ghosts."

"I see."

"Is there something you needed, Bonny?"

Bonny was obviously flustered, and for a moment seemed to have forgotten her purpose. After a long silence she managed to remember, and told Randall they were almost out of glass cleaner in the stockroom, and then she tried to leave in a hurry.

"Wait!" Penny was not going to let this opportunity pass. "Is there something you know of the ghost there?"

"I'm sorry Miss, I'm very busy."

"No, please tell me, is there something I should know if I'm to spend my wedding night there?"

Again Bonny gasped. "Your wedding night!"

"Yes, we're getting married on Valentine's Day."

With this news Bonny looked like she might faint. Penny guided her to one of the lobby wing chairs and Randall, somewhat amused at this point, brought her some water.

Bonny sat, but her hands were flailing in the air as her head swung back and forth. "You must change your plans, very bad juju if you don't."

"Juju?" Randall couldn't wait to hear more.

Bonny was no longer shy of speaking her mind. She was a large woman and now sat back comfortably in the lobby chair. She told them several stories of the hotel ghosts. Penny and Randall were both enthralled, leaning in and hanging on her every word. Bonny continued.

"And the worst of the worst…"—she paused, and looked them each in the eye—"is in Room 202. I should know. I've seen her—the ghost."

"Tell me everything." Penny couldn't believe her luck.

"I see her many time, mostly floating at the end of the bed. Oh she is so mournful, so sad. She wear a long white cloak and wanders around as if she is searching. So sorry I feel for her. If it was only that, I may have stay. But there was more, the windows would shatter for no reason, I see blood dripping down the walls, and that closet, THAT closet, it holds a bad spell, I'm sure of it."

Randall's eyes were bugged out at this point and his shoulders were tensed. With slow backwards steps, he tried to retreat back to the front desk. Without looking away from Bonny, Penny grabbed him by the wrist and pulled him back.

"That sounds truly terrifying," she said. "But tell me Bonny, how do you know so much about this?"

"Oh, when I first come to Winnipeg I work there. Not long, I tell you. Too many bad things." Her voice went to a whisper. "Once I was locked in that room. I don't know how she did it, but I sensed she wanted me to stay with her. I wished I could have maybe helped her, but I could not. I screamed and screamed until finally the other housekeeper hears me. She got me out. That the day I left."

"So you left there because of the ghosts and you came to work here!"

Penny and Randall exchanged knowing looks. Penny remembered the ghost at the Marlborough—Edith. How she had haunted the elevators, and how Steve had been assigned the very room Edith was murdered in so many years ago. She thought how all the events here had sparked her passion to begin writing her book on local ghosts.

"Yes, it's fine here. I did hear this hotel too had hauntings, but they in the past now. I sense nothing here. They must have found their way."

When the ghost of Edith had been murdered, the killer had taken her shoes. Penny had been sure that Edith wanted them back. Mostly to appease Penny, Steve did buy Edith a new pair of shoes. Together they had hid them for her under a loose floorboard in what had been Edith's room. It must have worked, Penny thought. Wait till I tell Steve.

Randall was nodding his head, "It's true Penny; we haven't had a problem with the elevators in a long time."

"So you see Miss, you must change your plans. And I will tell you why. I will tell you about the ghost of Room 202. She was a beautiful young bride-to-be, much like you, Miss."

Randall rolled his eyes at that comment. Penny elbowed him good-naturedly.

"She was to be married on February 14th, just like you again, but tragedy struck. Her fiancé met with a terrible accident, and he die. The young woman, she so overwhelmed by despair that she take her own life—hangs herself in the very closet in Room 202. They say she had hoped to join him in death. Sadly, she never did. She still look for him."

Penny gulped.

Bonny reached in her pocket and retrieved a small trinket. She pressed it into Penny's hand and closed her own hand tight over Penny's.

"I hope I have warned you enough, to stay away now. If not, please, keep this close, it will protect you." Bonny stood up and left, glancing back at Penny a few times with a worrisome look.

"Well that was lucky."

"Lucky? I don't know, Penny. You might be good to heed her advice."

"I meant it was lucky to bump into her and get all that information, for my book. But, yeah I hear you. I'm afraid it's too late to change any plans, though. Besides, Steve has promised not to leave me alone in the room for a minute."

"If you say so, Penny."

Penny couldn't wait to get back to work on her book with all the new information from Bonny. She had forgotten all about going to her parents to show them the dress. After she carefully hung it in the closet of the spare room, she nestled herself on the couch with her laptop. The first thing she wanted to do was confirm some of Bonny's stories. It took her a while, but she finally found a site about Winnipeg hauntings that held all the information she needed. She read intently the reports of guests hearing silverware rattling in cabinets and scratching sounds coming from dresser drawers. One housekeeper even claimed to have spotted the ghost of a young girl walking down the hallway and then vanishing into thin air. Just reading it made Penny feel all crawly. She wrapped her arms around herself and rubbed her shoulders nervously.

It was the folklore surrounding Room 202 that held Penny's fascination. It pretty much mirrored Bonny's words. She read how the maids had seen the walls literally bleed, and how they would find bloody footprints on the bed. How they would often find themselves locked in the room. Penny couldn't imagine how terrified she would be if she was ever locked alone in that room. Then she remembered how Naomi from the hotel had so much trouble with the key lock when she had shown them the room.

It was the window's shattering that really spooked her. The window had broken the day Steve proposed to her in that very room. They had blamed it on the wind, but now she wondered. Penny shuddered. Looking into the darkness just beyond the apartment window, she realized how late it had gotten. She hoped Steve would be home soon.

She continued reading. The story of the young bride-to-be was all there too, how it was said that she had hung herself in the closet, just as Bonny had told it. Again, she thought back to the day Steve proposed, how after the window had broken, the closet door had swung open and then slammed shut. Steve had blamed that on the wind too. At this point, Penny was beginning to truly regret that she had ever agreed to spend their wedding night in that room. Still, as terrifying as the ghostly bride sounded, Penny was overcome with compassion for her. She thought back to when Steve was in the hospital. How worried and despondent she had been. She wondered what lengths she would be driven to, had she lost him. It made her so grateful for the beautiful wedding she and Steve had to look forward to. It seemed so unfair that the young bride from the past had been cheated of not only her wedding, but also of her whole future. So engrossed, Penny never even heard when Steve came in. Except for the glow of her laptop, the apartment had grown dark, as nightfall had descended.

Seeing that Penny hadn't heard him come in, Steve took a moment to just stop and look at her. She looked so small sitting in the corner of the couch with her legs tucked under. She was so intent on her work that he hated to disturb her. He quietly walked over to the couch and stood behind her. Not wanting to interrupt her concentration, he gently put a hand on her shoulder, just to let her know he was home.

Penny shrieked and leaped off the couch. The laptop flew on the floor. Steve stood back in disbelief.

"It's just me Pen, what's with you."

As she leaped into his arms a smirk began to form on his face, he had scared her silly! But when he felt her shivering in his arms he changed his tune. Not knowing where any of this was coming from, he simply held her close.

"Oh Steve! There is no way we can stay in THAT room for our wedding."

Now Steve understood what this was all about; Penny had somehow managed to really spook herself.

"Sure we can, Pen. I'll be there with you the whole time, there's nothing to be afraid of."

With her face buried in his shirt she began to sniffle and sob.

Still holding her close, Steve shuffled them both just close enough to the table to grab a few tissues out of the box. He offered them to her.

Between heavy sobs she blew her nose—very loudly, to Steve's surprise.

CHAPTER NINETEEN

Friday, February 14, 2014

"I, Steven, take you, uh, Penny, for my lawful wife, to have and to hold, from this day forward, um, for better, for worse, for richer, for poorer, in sickness and health, until death do us part."

"You sound too nervous, Steve. Try it again, put a little feeling in it this time."

"Oh come on, Randall, this is stupid. I'm not rehearsing for a play. It's my goddamn wedding."

Randall had never heard of anyone practising their vows before the service, but he thought it was an ingenious way to get Steve to stop pacing for a while. "Take it easy Steve, you're too stressed. It's just a little wedding."

"No it's not. It's a big-ass wedding at the Hotel Fort Gary. Why did I want such a stupid big wedding? Penny just wanted something small."

Randall was taking his best man duties seriously. He was doing his best to calm Steve down and make sure everything went well. This unnerved Steve all the more; he would have appreciated if the real Randall was there to make fun and tease relentlessly as usual. A poke in the ribs at this point would have been welcomed.

"I give up. For a big, tough-guy detective you sure are being a big baby about all this. Let's go see Penny. If anyone can talk some sense into you it's her."

"Isn't there some rule about seeing her before the wedding?"

"That's true Steve; they say its' bad luck. And you know me, I'm not one to risk breaking superstitions, but I'm desperate. You've been a wreck all morning."

"All right, let's go. Pen and her mom are in Room 202 getting ready. If I'm this nervous she's likely way worse. She'll probably need me to calm her down!"

They headed down the hallway and as they approached the door to Room 202 they heard laughter. They both recognized Penny's distinctive laugh.

"Yeah, Steve." Randall rolled his eyes. "She sounds like she's a real mess."

Randall put up his arm in front of Steve. "You stay here." He lifted the knocker and banged it three times.

Penny opened the door a crack and peered through at him. "What do you want?"

Penny had some kind of mask on her face and her hair was wound in large rollers. She wore a white terry towel robe.

Randall whispered through the crack in the door. "It's Steve, Penny, he's a wreck. I can't handle him anymore. Please talk to him."

Penny touched her hands to her rollers and began to laugh again. "Tell him to come on in."

Steve pushed past Randall, nudged him and whispered, "I told you, she's hysterical. Good thing we came."

Randall begged Penny's mom to come and help him with his tie. She was more than happy to help and didn't let on, even if she did know, that it was merely a ploy to give Penny and Steve a moment alone.

Steve stood staring at Penny in her rollers and face mask. "Well, I finally understand why it's bad luck for the groom to see the bride before the wedding."

Penny sat on the vanity stool and leaned close to the mirror. She proceeded to vigorously rub the mask off with a wet facecloth. "Well no worries, this will be the last time my hair sees rollers, or I let my mom talk me into another one of these silly face masks."

Steve sat on the end of the bed and watched her with amusement. Her back was to him, but he could see her face in the mirror, scrunching as she fought to remove the mask. Randall was right, he thought; it was a good idea to come see Penny. He felt better, relaxed. Penny closed her eyes and ran the facecloth over them to get the last bit off. It was then that Steve felt a cool rush of air slip by him. He looked in the mirror and was astounded to see a beautiful young bride with bouncy blond curls and red lips stare back at him. Steve knew for sure it wasn't Penny's reflection. The bride smiled at him. While his mind tried to rationalize what he was seeing, the bride's smiling face changed. Her eyes shut and her beautiful red lips turned to blood and began to drip down the corners of her mouth. Before Steve could react to what he thought he was seeing, a loud thud inside the closet jolted him. Penny's eyes popped open and the other bride's image vanished.

"What was that?" Penny asked.

Steve was already up and rushing towards the closet door. He pulled the door open fast, as if he expected something to jump out.

At his feet was an iron, its cord still attached to the board affixed to the door.

"Oh, it's just the iron. That spooked me out for a second. You OK, Steve? You look a little pale."

"No, I'm good, just a few pre-wedding jitters." He decided it best not to mention what he saw in the mirror, since it was likely just his nerves and overactive imagination. Boy, he thought, this getting-married stuff sure does a number on a guy! "I think I'll go find Randall."

"Oh no you won't! A promise is a promise. I only agreed to stay in this room as long as I'm never left alone. You wait until my mom gets back now."

Steve would have normally ribbed her about her irrational fear of ghosts, but given what just happened, he said nothing and stayed.

CHAPTER TWENTY

"I, Penny, take you, Steven, for my lawful husband, to have and to hold, from this day forward, for better, for worse, for richer, for poorer, in sickness and health, until death do us part."

Steve could not believe this beautiful woman was saying these words to him. He gasped when she had arrived in the small hotel chapel. Stunning was the only word that came to mind. He could tell by the smirk she gave him when she entered, that she too knew how fabulous she looked. Her dress flowed and clung naturally to her slender curves. It was a beautiful dress, yet understated enough to leave Penny as the showpiece. Her face glowed, her eyes dazzled and her skin shimmered.

A soft poke from Randall cued Steve to pay attention. It was time to kiss the bride. The room was full of guests, but once pronounced husband and wife, they kissed like they were the only two people in the room. It was the most gentle, loving kiss they had ever shared, and it went on and on. It went on so long that the guests were beginning to fidget. Some snickered quietly. Some began to look slightly uncomfortable, including Penny's mom, who smiled graciously at the guests and at one point lifted her hands in an apologetic fashion. When they finally came up for air Penny looked up at Steve, her face flushed.

"Now there's my blushing bride."

To the relief of everyone, especially the pianist who had been sitting with fingers poised for some time, they made their way down the aisle to cheers, applause and a resounding piano piece.

Later at the reception, Penny said, "Let's go dance."

She had made a few surprising discoveries about her new husband. First of all he looked terrific in a tux, and secondly, he was a superb dancer.

"Not again! You're going to wear me out before we even get to the room tonight."

When Steve heard the song playing, he stopped protesting. It was an old hit, one of their favourites. Frankie's velvet voice crooned from the DJ's speakers. "I'll be seeing you, in all the old, familiar places, that this heart of mine embrace, all day through..." As they expertly manoeuvered the dance floor Penny looked up at Steve. "Where did you learn to dance so well?"

"My mom, actually. She claimed my dad was the most exquisite dancer. She joked that it was why she married him—and why she stayed married to him. She insisted my brother and I learn too. We spent many Saturday nights as kids with the coffee table moved out of the way, and the records would spin all evening."

"It was a perfect day, wasn't it?"

"It was, but I have to admit, I'm relieved the hard part is over."

She laid her head on his chest. "Me too."

The song ended and they headed toward the champagne fountain. A small group was assembled there, including Randall and Rose. Penny reached for a champagne flute and filled it. Thirsty from dancing, she gulped it down quite quickly.

"Everything was just beautiful, Penny."

"Thank you, Rose. Isn't this room fabulous?"

They looked up at the high ceilings, the glittery chandeliers. The tables had been covered with white tablecloths and each chair was covered with rose-coloured linen, and gathered expertly at the back. Clear crystal vases held bouquets of pink and white roses at every table.

"The whole hotel is fabulous!" Rose said. "Such character! Perfect choice for your wedding."

"Isn't it, though."

"I read it was built way back in 1913. Isn't that a miracle, over a hundred years old now and still so grand! Did you know it was once the tallest building in the city?"

"No, but I just find the whole place wildly romantic. Makes me wonder how many other weddings took place here. Who they were and what were their stories?"

"Well that's the writer in you coming out, Penny. How is your book coming?"

"Honestly, I haven't even opened my laptop for weeks. After the wedding, though, I'll get back to it. I was actually hoping for some inspiration here, especially in our supposedly haunted room, but nothing. The iron fell in the closet—that was it. No ghost story there."

Rose laughed. "I don't know, Penny. I find irons pretty scary, vacuums too. I'm not much for housework."

"Well, taking care of three young children can't be easy."

"You said it. Just keeping them fed and in clean clothes is enough. Thankfully Randall isn't afraid of helping out. Especially now."

"Now?"

Rose smiled and placed both hands gently on her belly. "I didn't want to say anything earlier, but baby number four, on the way."

Penny hugged her. "How wonderful! Congratulations Rose. Can this day get any better? Wait until I tell Steve, where did he go now?"

Rose excused herself and headed to the ladies room. Penny refilled her champagne flute and glanced about the room for Steve. She couldn't wait to tell him Rose and Randall's news. Scanning the room, she realized she knew very few of their guests. They were either friends of her mother's, people Steve knew from work or his relatives or family friends. She knew he had been disappointed that his brother couldn't make it in from Vancouver, but it really was short notice.

It didn't take long to spot him. With his looming height, Steve wasn't all that hard to pick out in a crowd. He was off in a corner, talking to Grant. They looked to be in a serious discussion, so she decided not to interrupt. As she sipped her champagne she spotted Randall, and headed over to congratulate him instead.

Grant had been ordering a beer at the bar when Steve came up beside him. Grant slapped Steve solidly on the back. "Congratulations again, Steve. You got yourself one hell of a nice lady there."

"Thanks Grant. Where's Angel? I haven't had a chance to thank her for coming."

Grant took a long sip of his beer, "You're too late. She left."

"Left? I thought you were staying the night. Did she go up to the room?"

"Nope, gone home. Said she had one of her migraine headaches, wanted to be in her own bed."

"Did she drive? Is she OK?"

"Oh, she's fine. I don't even know if I believe the headache story. I put her in a cab out front. I'm still staying the night. I plan on having a couple of beer, so I won't be driving."

"I'm real sorry she left, Grant. I know you were hoping tonight would work out differently."

"What are you going to do, eh?" Grant took another sip of his beer, smiled and winked at Steve. "Now let's go find your beautiful bride, I haven't had the honour of a dance yet."

Steve smiled too and put his arm around Grant's shoulder. "Good idea, my friend. Let's go find her."

By about midnight most of the guests had filtered out. Penny had been sipping champagne all evening and was a bit giddy. If she didn't know all her guests by the start of the evening, she did by the end. She had also done a fair bit of dancing, and Steve loved seeing her enjoying herself, mingling with everyone, having a genuine good time. He sometimes worried she spent too much time alone with her nose in her laptop. She was across the hall chatting with a group of her mother's friends when he caught her trying to stifle a yawn. He knew then it was likely a good time to make their exit.

Except for Randall and Rose, embraced closely for a slow song, the dance floor was empty. Steve strode across it toward Penny. She stopped and watched him—so tall and handsome. He smiled charmingly to the ladies and placed his hand flat against the small of Penny's back. He leaned over and whispered, "You almost ready to go, Pen?"

Penny looked up at him, smiled and nodded.

"Excuse us."

They tried to sneak out, but the DJ caught them and announced their departure. "Ladies and gentlemen, let's bid the new happy couple goodnight, sleep tight."

Penny and Steve stopped at the doorway, turned back and waved at the last of their guests. It was all very nice until the DJ blasted out the song, "Wild thing, you make my heart sing…"

Rose and Randall picked up the pace on the dance floor. So did Steve and Penny as they dashed out.

It wasn't until they were in the elevator alone that Steve realized how much champagne she had actually consumed. She was more brazen than she had ever been with him. Pushing him into the corner of the small confines of the elevator, she pressed her body hard against him. Steve couldn't help but smile and wonder how the rest of the night might go. "Be gentle with me," he teased.

Just as he went to press their floor button the elevator dinged.

The doors opened and an elderly couple entered. Steve had managed to push Penny away just in time, but considering their attire, he was sure he had fooled no one. The number two lit up on the display and the doors opened. Steve was relieved to make their exit. The couple smiled knowingly at them as the doors closed.

Their room wasn't far from the elevator, and once safely inside, Steve found that not only did the champagne make Penny forward; it also caused her to lose her usual fears. After she slipped out of dress she swung open the closet, poked her head inside and hollered, "Any ghosts in here? Pardon me if there is, just hanging up my dress." She laughed as she said it and turned to smile at Steve. He stood in awe, not only because of her newfound bravery, but also the sheer sight of her. The removal of her dress had revealed the sexiest lingerie he had ever seen her wear. White lace and silk clung to her body, leaving little to the imagination. Her legs glimmered in old-style nylons, held up with a feathery white garter. She had really gone all out for this sultry surprise.

Steve smirked. "You shouldn't make fun of ghosts, Pen. Randall says it's never a good idea."

Penny threw herself on the bed and struck a seductive pose. "You coming to bed, or what?"

"You bet I am."

Steve removed his tux and, threw it on the floor. "Just give me a minute," he said as he disappeared into the bathroom.

He wasn't gone long, but when he returned, his sultry bride had rolled over and was already sound asleep.

"Penny, wake up!" He shook her gently, then a little harder.

Nothing.

"Come on Penny, wake up, it's our wedding night!"

When the slightest, most dainty snoring began, he gave up. Well, it was almost a perfect day, he thought, smiling. It wasn't long before he too was fast asleep.

CHAPTER TWENTY-ONE

Steve lay rigid in the hotel bed. The only discernible movement lay just below his closed eyelids, where rapid and jerky motion caused chaos with his subconscious. His dreams had forced his eye's view inwards, and it was there that the blood flowed. At first, from his leg, pools of it soaked the sheets of the bed. He knew exactly what to do—wrap the wound tight, stop the bleeding. It was his only chance. The problem was, he couldn't move. He was frozen still. Only his eyes moved, and as his gaze darted around the room he saw the broken window. The snow was blowing in.

That was when he saw her, the bride—his bride. It was Penny, standing at the window, looking out. He wondered why she just stood there. She must be cold. As if she had heard his thoughts she turned slowly to look at him. Fear seized him when he saw it wasn't Penny. He struggled to move, but couldn't. He looked at her face. It was the bride from inside the mirror. Her blond curls were blown askew and her eyes were downcast, but he knew it was her. Blood drizzled from the corners of her mouth and flowed from the gashes on her wrists. With her head tilted to one side, she held her bleeding arms up and floated toward him.

"Heeelp meeeeeee," she whispered.

Steve was in anguish now. He had to get up to help her…

She floated past him and into the closet.

The closet door slammed shut behind her.

Steve felt warm now and discovered he could move. He was awake! The room had warmed too, and beads of sweat dripped off his face. He was relieved to be able to move, and he got out of the bed. He was relieved it had just been a dream. He looked over at Penny. She was still fast asleep. He headed to the washroom to throw some cold water on his face, but hesitated at the closet door. Damn iron must have fallen again, that's probably what woke him from his nightmare. He was thankful it did. He opened the closet door to pick it up.

Steve froze. There she was again, the mystery bride. This time she hung limply from the closet rod.

Steve screamed, but no sound came out.

The bride's head hung limply to one side. He could barely see her face. Despite his fear he knew he had to find out who she was. Hesitantly he slowly reached in the closet. He brushed aside her blond curls and gently lifted her chin up so he could see her face.

It was not the bride from the mirror! Glaring out at him with a huge smile and eyes wide open was the face of an angel—an Angel he happened to know. Her face was so bright, almost blinding—and beautiful, except for a harsh bruise on the one side of her face. He quickly let go, pulled his hand away and shut the door.

His cellphone on the bedside table began to chirp.

Steve opened his eyes to find himself back in bed. The cellphone had stopped chirping, but had started up again. He was breathing heavily as he reached for the phone.

"Yeah?"

"Steve, it's Dan."

Steve rubbed his eyes, glanced at the empty closet and sat up. Now really awake, he realized that he had just been having a nightmare. There was no bride in the room but his, and no angel in the closet.

"Chief Dan?"

"Yeah, I need you to come down to the lobby."

"What? Now?"

"Yes, I need—"

"It's my wedding night, for Christ's sake!"

"Pronto!"

"Be right there."

Steve hung up the phone.

"Penny, I got to go." He gave her a nudge.

The phone hadn't woken her.

He got up and stood by Penny's side of the bed. He gently shook her. "Penny, wake up, I've got to go down to the lobby." He shook her a bit harder.

Nothing, no response. She was sound asleep.

He was torn what to do. He had promised not to leave her alone, but Chief Dan had said 'pronto,' their code for don't ask any questions, just come immediately. He considered calling Randall to come, but dismissed that thought. It was too late, and he didn't have time to wait anyway. Likely, he'd be back before she woke. If not, he would call Randall to come to the room. He grabbed his cellphone, pulled the covers over Penny's bare shoulder and then, just before he left, he looked at the open closet. He went over and shut the door.

Steve made his way down the stairs as quick as he could with his bum leg. There was no time to wait for an elevator. When he reached the lobby he was surprised to find so much activity—strange, he thought, for this time of night. He noticed there were quite a few uniforms mulling about too. He looked for Chief Dan. The chief saw Steve first and rushed toward him.

"Steve, come with me."

"What the hell's going on?"

Chief Dan didn't answer. He gently held Steve's arm and guided him to a small alcove in the lobby. It was a private spot with a few comfortable couches and chairs. It looked like it could be a living room in an older upscale home.

"Sit down, Steve."

Steve remained standing. "Come on, Dan, I promised Penny I wouldn't leave her alone. Now please, tell me what's going on."

"It's Grant."

"Grant! What about him?"

There was no way to soften it, no way to delay it.

"He's dead, Steve."

CHAPTER TWENTY-TWO

Penny's eyes fluttered open and she smiled. She was lying on her side, facing the window. She noticed it was still dark; a few stars sparkled in the distant sky. Her head felt fuzzy but still, she felt wonderful. Even though she had fallen asleep on her new husband, on their wedding night, still she knew everything was OK. It was better than OK, and they had their whole life to make up for the one night they missed.

As she stretched her arms in the air, she also suddenly realized that she had actually—well, almost—spent the whole night in the so-called haunted room at the Hotel Fort Garry! Maybe she could write harrowing ghost stories after all. Had she not proven her bravery, faced her fears by staying in this room? Granted, she couldn't have done it without Steve. Still, it was quite a feat for her.

She could feel the weight of him lying beside her on the bed. Her back was turned away from him and she wondered why he was not cuddled close to her, why his one arm wasn't draped over her. It was how they usually slept, and she found it ever so comforting. Was he upset she fell asleep or was he just really tired?

"Steve?"

She tried again.

He made no reply, and there was her answer, he must be beat. She shut her eyes to go back to sleep, but her mouth was dry so she decided to get up and get some water. Slipping quietly out of bed, so as not to wake Steve she tip-toed in the dark room and headed to the washroom. Once inside, she flicked on the light and squinted at its brightness. On the counter were two clean glasses wrapped in paper. Knowing what a light sleeper Steve was, she opened one as quietly as she could. Still every crinkly sound resounded loudly and she was sure he'd wake up.

Catching a glimpse of herself in the mirror she was amused at her reflection, still dressed for romance. Now she secretly hoped Steve would wake up. She purposely left the light on as she made her exit, hoping the brightness might rouse him. It worked. Steve was no longer lying on the bed. The light from the washroom only partially illuminated the bed; the rest of the room was still quite dark. Her eyes tried to adjust to the darkness as they darted around the room to see where he was.

"Steve?"

"Steve, where are you!"

She was almost ready to panic, until she saw him. There he stood at the end of the bed. She couldn't really see him—just his shape in the dark. He was standing very still.

"There you are. You almost scared me to death!"

Penny reached down to turn on the bedside lamp. The light cast a soft glow and she turned to look up and smile at Steve.

He was gone!

Oh my God, oh my God! Where is he? If he were playing a joke on her, she would not be hanging around to find out! She threw open the closet door to grab a housecoat.

The damn iron fell again.

She dropped the housecoat and ran out the door.

While Penny stood alone in the hallway she forced herself to think of the best thing to do. It was too late to wake anybody, and she didn't feel like wandering the halls alone. Where was Steve? Why the hell did he leave her alone? The only thing she could think to do was head to the lobby. It would be embarrassing in her honeymoon outfit but it was late, likely no one around. It was really her only option; she was not going back to that room. At least in the lobby she could use the phone, try to call Steve on his cell. If that didn't work she'd call Randall, even if it were late. She pressed the elevator down button. The car arrived quickly. Alone in the elevator, she noticed her feet were bare, and her hands were trembling.

The news of Grant's death had hit Steve hard. He could not believe it. He had just talked with Grant a few hours ago at the wedding. When Chief Dan had told him, the colour had drained from his face. He sat down and buried his face in his hands, and then ran his fingers through his hair. "No, it must be a mistake! This can't be true!"

When Chief Dan assured him it was very true, Steve snapped out of it. He knew he did not have time to grieve or question anything right now. He had to put his personal reactions aside and do his job. It's all he could do for Grant now, pursue an investigation into what the hell happened.

"OK, let's go. Where is he?"

"He's in his car, in the underground parking. I'm real sorry, Steve. It looks like he shot himself with his own gun."

"No. That can't be. Something sounds off, Chief. He told me he was staying here tonight. Said he was having a few beers at the wedding. I know Grant; he wasn't going anywhere, he wouldn't be in his car."

As hard as he was trying to be professional, Steve had to turn his face away for a moment to gain some composure.

"Do you know where his wife is, Steve? Angel, is it? A few officers went up to their room. She wasn't there."

Steve headed towards the parking area and Chief Dan followed.

"She had a headache. Grant said she wanted to go home, be in her own bed. Said he called her a cab. That was before midnight. Oh shit!"

"What Steve, what is it, did you remember something else?"

"No, sorry, just Penny. I left her sleeping in the room. She'll freak if she wakes up and I'm not there."

"She'll be fine. You want me to send an officer up to tell her—"

A loud commotion back in the lobby caused them both to turn around.

And there she stood, just outside the elevator doors—his beautiful bride, wearing only her honeymoon lingerie and looking totally embarrassed. Despite the severity and sombre turn of events, an amused smile crossed over Steve's face. It didn't last. He rushed over to her.

"Why did you leave me alone?" she yelled. "Why are there so many people here?"

"Shush, it's OK, Penny." A uniform passed Steve his jacket and Steve helped her put it on. Every eye in the crowded lobby was on them.

Penny saw now that everyone was watching, and she knew enough to stop screaming at him. Instead she grabbed him by his shirt, pulled him closer and whispered, not gently, "You promised not to leave me alone in there! Why the hell did you leave me? I am never going to—"

"Steve? Steve! We found something."

"Pen, I'm sorry, I have to go."

"Go? Where are you…?"

Chief Dan motioned for Steve to go with the other officer and assured him he'd take care of Penny.

Chief Dan wrapped an arm around her, "Come on Penny, I'll get one of the officers to take you back to your room. He can stay until you call someone if you want."

"Thank you, but no, there's no bloody way I'm going back in that room. What the hell is going on?"

"Maybe I should let Steve tell you, it's just that…"

"No, please, you tell me! Tell me now!"

Chief Dan filled Penny in on the horrific events that had taken place. As she listened in disbelief her legs became wobbly and Chief Dan had to steady her when she looked ready to topple over. He guided her to a chair and helped her sit down.

"I know this is a horrible shock and I'm really sorry Penny, but I do have to get over there. Is there someone I can call to take you to your room?"

"Of course, I mean, NO! I can't go back there Dan." Her hands trembled as she tried to explain.

"There was someone in my room, they were in my bed!"

"Okay, okay", he held both her hands in his, "I'll have some officer's go check it out. Did you see them? Was it a man or a woman?"

"No, you don't understand. It wasn't someone; it was more of a something." Penny was becoming hysterical. "They were in my bed, then just standing there—and then they disappeared!"

Chief Dan was losing his patience now and kept glancing towards the parking garage. "Oh Penny, I think you've just got the jitters from all the stories about that room. You'll be safe with the officer, I'll make sure he checks the room real well before you go in, but I really have to go."

Realizing how ridiculous her stories must sound in the wake of the tragic events, Penny took a deep breath. "No, I mean yes, of course, you go. Tell Steve I'm really sorry, I'll be fine. I'll call Randall to come down and get me. I'll go to their room, no go, just go." Penny gave him a gentle push.

He did leave, but not before he sent over an officer to stay with her.

When Chief Dan arrived in the underground parking he could see Steve had everything under control. He always admired how Steve worked. There were no short cuts; everything was done right. No piece of evidence dared hide from Steve.

Dan handed Steve a cup of coffee he had quickly grabbed on the way. He hadn't bothered putting anything in it. Steve took a big sip and barely noticed how it burned his mouth and throat on the way down.

"They found his cellphone. Looks like it fell under his seat." Steve held up a plastic Ziploc bag that now held Grant's phone.

"Good, good. Anything else?"

"Not yet, but we're still collecting evidence. We've secured the building. No one gets in or out without us knowing. We're also monitoring the hallways for anything suspicious."

"That's good. Steve, but do you really think it's necessary? Looks like it was a suicide."

"For Christ's sake, Dan, you know as well as me, things aren't always what they appear. A murderer could be still in the hotel. Where's Penny?"

"Take it easy Steve, she's fine. I left an officer with her. She's going to call Randall."

"Good, now leave me to do my job."

Chief Dan held up both his hands, palms open toward Steve. "OK, OK, sorry." He backed away and watched over the process.

Steve continued to take part, as well as oversee the evidence gathering. He tried not to look at Grant, sitting there in his car, sitting there like Steve had seen him many times before, only not dead, not like this.

CHAPTER TWENTY-THREE

"This is the worst part of the job."

"Yeah, it sure is, Steve."

Chief Dan and Steve were heading to Grant's house to give Angel the news.

"Funny she hasn't called his cell looking for him."

"Why would she, Steve? Wasn't he supposed to stay at the hotel?"

"Yeah, but I had one of the officers check his phone and there was a text from her, shortly before the estimated time of death."

"Really? What did it say?"

"She told him to come home, said they needed to talk."

"Well that would explain why he was in his car."

"Yeah, exactly, but why would he go to his car to go see her, but before he leaves he decides to pull his gun out and shoot himself? It just doesn't make any sense."

"I know Steve, this is a tough one for you, but people do strange things. Maybe he intended to go see her and then just couldn't face it. Who knows what was going on between them?"

At that, Steve went quiet. He regretted not sharing what Grant told him about hitting Angel. If it was suicide, Steve blamed himself. The guy must have had more problems than he had realized. He probably needed some serious help, and Steve should have known, should have insisted on it.

They rode the rest of the way in silence. The only sound was the car heat blowing at full blast. It had been one of the coldest winters Winnipeg had seen in a very long time. They had also had a record amount of snow fall and the whole city was fed-up shoveling their way out of their driveways. Daylight had just begun, and as they drove down the road to Grant's home the streetlights turned off. Chief Dan was just about to pull in the driveway when Steve said, "Stop."

He pointed to fresh tire tracks in the driveway, and Chief Dan knew then to park on the road. They saw a light on in the kitchen as they got out of the car. They walked across the street and Steve removed his gloves and pulled out his cellphone to quickly snap a picture of the tire tracks. He would have rather waited, in case Angel was looking out the window, but he couldn't take the chance the tracks would be disturbed, or that another fresh snowfall would cover them. Chief Dan was already at the front door and Steve ran to catch up. They took one last look at each other and then Chief Dan pressed the doorbell.

Angel peeked through the window to see who was there before unlocking and opening the door. She smiled suspiciously at them.

"Good morning, what brings you gentlemen out so early? Come on in, I've got coffee on in the kitchen."

Steve's heart was breaking for her. Her blond hair was tied back in a loose ponytail and her face revealed no makeup, yet she looked even more beautiful than ever. She was wearing a creamy white sweatsuit that did little to hide her curves. Steve understood how Grant was so taken with her. They followed her into the kitchen.

Steve started to tell her but couldn't finish, "Angel, we, uh..." He turned away.

Angel set her coffee cup down on the table and covered her mouth with both hands.

She looked directly at Steve. "Oh no, it's your wedding night, something awful must have happened!"

Steve and Dan watched as she slowly lowered herself onto a chair and looked up at them, searchingly.

Chief Dan pulled up a chair across from her. He held both her hands and did his best to break the news to her gently.

When he was finished, Angel said nothing. She pulled her hands away and hung them by her side. She looked blankly around the kitchen for a long moment. Finally, she got up and walked over to the fridge. On the door, held by a magnet, was a photo of Grant and her. In the background was a beach, and they both looked tanned. It looked like they were on a vacation; they had big smiles. Angel reached up and touched the picture. She ran her finger along Grant's face. She turned to look at Steve. "It's my worst fear. Is he really gone, Steve?"

Steve rushed over to her. She looked like she might collapse, so he wrapped his arms around her to hold her. He tried to lead her back to sit down, but she hung on to him. Hung on for dear life and sobbed quietly. Her perfume from the night before still lingered, and Steve breathed it in. It should have been a great night for her and Grant, a romantic night to forget their problems. What went wrong!

CHAPTER TWENTY-FOUR

It may have been the worst wedding night ever, but Steve knew he had married the best wife imaginable. She managed to take care of everything while he was busy with the investigation and gone to give Angel the horrible news. Their wedding gifts sat unwrapped in their apartment storage, and she knew where her new husband's priorities lay. When he got home she sat up with him for hours, filling his coffee cup over and over. She knew he was tired and would eventually need some rest so, unknown to him at the time, she brewed decaf. She let him talk it all out. She already knew about Grant and Angel's money problems and how Angel was slipping off to the out-of-town bar, but she didn't know Grant had hit her. When Steve told her, she was shocked, but she didn't react. She wanted to be calm; she knew she was only a sounding board at the moment.

Grant's suicide made sense to her now. Financial trouble, marital problems, guilt over the fact he hit her, and then seeing how happy Steve and Penny were—it must have been too much for him. To have Angel leave that night, instead of staying at the hotel must have been the final trigger. A few drinks probably didn't help the situation either. It was obvious what happened here, yet Steve didn't believe it, or couldn't.

Penny never voiced her opinion. She just listened. When Steve asked her if she would mind if he went back to work right away instead taking the time off they had planned, she told him to go. She knew he needed to. She was worried, though. Steve was so sure Grant wouldn't have done it, but it was so clear he had. She would be there for him when he finally exhausted every bit of evidence and had to admit the truth. Until then, she would just listen.

Chief Dan pleaded with Steve to take the time off for the honeymoon. He figured Steve needed it now more than ever after what happened with Grant. Steve wouldn't hear of it. He was still convinced it wasn't suicide. He realized it looked like he was in denial, but that wasn't it, he knew Grant wouldn't do that, and he intended to prove it.

He had to admit that Chief Dan did have a point about the time off. It was hard being back. The worst thing about it was facing the sight of Grant's empty desk. His coffee cup still sat where he left it, as if waiting for Grant's return. A few of the guys offered to clean up Grant's desk, but Steve was adamant that it be left as it is. He used the excuse that he needed to go through any paperwork, but in reality he couldn't stand to have him or anyone touch a thing. That would make it all too real. It would make it look like Grant really wasn't coming back. Steve sat at his own desk, unable to concentrate, wondering when, if ever, he'd be able to clear Grant's desk.

Another tough part about being back was how everyone was so nice to him. He secretly always hoped for this, but not now, not because of this. He hated it. It was such bullshit. Even Buddy stopped by his desk, offered condolences and asked Steve if he wanted to join him for lunch later. Before Steve could come up with an excuse a courier dropped a package at his desk. He was relieved to see it was from the hotel and obviously the security tapes he'd requested.

"Thanks for the invite, Buddy." He pointed at the package and even smiled. "But it looks like I'm going to be busy for a while." The smile was genuine. He was glad the tapes arrived, for they not only given him an excuse to get out of lunch, but also allowed him a good excuse to hoard himself up alone in the conference room.

Steve stood and grabbed the package and picked up a coffee on the way. Once in the conference room he felt like he could breathe again. He shut the door and prepared to immerse himself in his work. He put in the first tape and leaned back in the chair. He cringed when after only a few minutes of tape, he realized much of the footage would include his own wedding guests' comings and goings. He reached for a piece of paper off the conference room table and pulled a pen out of his shirt pocket, ready to make any notations.

He barely got started when he heard the click of the conference room door open.

"Hey Steve, can I come in a moment?"

It was Phil Cleaver, the department shrink.

Steve sighed. "Sure, come on in, Phil, flick on the light."

Phil pulled up a chair, sat backwards on it and leaned forward toward Steve.

"It's been a while, Phil, how ya been?"

"I'm good Steve, same ol', same ol'. What I'm more concerned about is how are you?"

"Chief Dan send you?"

"Well when I heard what happened to your partner, I was going to make a point of calling you anyway, but yeah, Dan was concerned, wanted me to come have a chat with you."

"Grant. My partner's name was Grant."

"Of course, yes, Steve, and I'm so very sorry. And, Steve, bad time to mention it but, really, congratulations on your wedding."

Steve knew what a visit from Phil meant, and it wasn't a social call. Phil was there to assess him, and if he didn't pass, he was off on leave—again. He decided if he was going to solve Grant's murder, which he was sure it was, he'd have to be at work, for he needed the resources. It was bullshit time.

"Yes, thank you Phil, on both accounts. I didn't work with him long, but he was one of the good ones. I'm really going to miss him."

"Of course you are, and how are you handling that?"

"I have to admit, it's not easy, but don't worry, I'll be OK."

"I hope you don't mind, Steve, but I talked to some of the guys, they said you insisted no one touch a thing on Grant's desk. Why is that?"

"Oh it's not what you think. We were working on a case. I need to go through his notes and the paperwork; I just don't want anything thrown out that might be pertinent. You know what a stickler I am for details." Steve even managed a smile.

"Well that makes sense. Now Dan tells me it was obviously a suicide. I hear you don't agree, Steve. Can you tell me why?"

"Oh, don't get me wrong, if anyone can read the evidence and see the writing on the wall it's me, Phil. I know, too, that Grant was having some personal problems, so yeah, it all fits. Dan must have misunderstood why I was following through with this. What kind of homicide detective would I be Phil, if I didn't investigate all angles to just be a hundred per cent sure? I owe Grant at least that."

"You're a good man Steve. Keep up the good work and if you have any concerns, you make sure you call me, OK?"

Phil pulled a business card out of his pocket and handed it to Steve.

"I'll do that, Phil, and thanks for the talk."

Phil stopped on his way out the door and looked back at Steve, "Good job Steve, you passed another assessment." He smiled wryly, flicked out the light and shut the door.

Steve exhaled a long, slow breath, took a sip of cold coffee and turned the security tapes back on. Instead of concentrating on the tapes, he recalled the last assessment with Phil. It seemed so long ago. That assessment meant a series of talks; Steve gave all the right answers that time, too.

He sat up straight, gulped the last of the cold coffee and hit rewind. He started with the footage from the underground parking, but he had requested all tapes from that fateful night. Concentrating, combing over all the evidence, beginning with those tapes, was crucial. He'd scoured security tapes many times before; it was tedious work, but if you let your guard down, you could miss something important.

Steve thought he caught sight of something unusual on the tape. He hit stop and rewind. When he played it back it was nothing. This was a common occurrence when viewing these tapes, he continued watching intently.

There was a tapping.

Steve continued watching.

The tapping continued.

"What the hell!" Steve pressed the stop button again and got up to see what the annoying tapping sound was. It couldn't be the door; people usually just barged in, and if they did knock, it was loudly.

It was the door. Frustrated, he lunged at it and pulled it open fast. It hit the wall stopper with a thud. "What now, for Chri—"

Standing very still and ever so contrite was the beautiful Angel.

"I'm so sorry to disturb you Steve, I can go…"

"Oh God, Angel, don't be sorry, I'm sorry, I didn't know it was you, please, come on in."

Steve flicked on the light and then pulled out a chair for her. She shook her head. "I'd rather stand if you don't mind."

"No, no, not at all, I…"

He didn't know what to say. He just stood there staring at her. Her eyes were swollen and red. Other than that, she looked impeccable. Her blond hair was pulled back, and she wore a warm camel coat over tight black pants with a black turtleneck. Her skin was flawless and it glowed softly, even in the stark fluorescent lighting.

Angel glanced at the screen; it displayed the parking garage of the Hotel Fort Garry. She gasped.

"Oh shit, I'm sorry." Steve ran and quickly turned it off.

Angel sat down now. "I just can't believe he's gone, Steve."

"I know, I know. I can't, either."

"It's all my fault. I drove him to this, Steve."

"No Angel, you were the brightest spot in his life. He loved you so much. He would hate for you to say that."

"It's true, there's so much you don't know."

"I probably know more than you think."

Angel looked up at Steve, lifting her long thick lashes and peering at him with her big blue eyes. "No Steve, I'm sure there is a lot you don't know."

Steve pulled his own chair closer to hers and put his hand gently on top of hers, "Well then, why don't you tell me."

She did, and she was right. There was a lot he hadn't known.

CHAPTER TWENTY-FIVE

Penny sat on the couch, staring once again at the blank screen of her laptop. She thought some writing might take her mind off things. She also wanted to capture what had happened to her in that room on her wedding night. She knew there had been someone, or something, lying beside her on the bed. It fit too, with stories that other guests had told. Her fingers were poised at the keyboard, but they were motionless.

She thought back to that night, how she had managed to make such a fool of herself showing up in the lobby. Imagine how silly all Steve's co-workers must have thought his new wife to be, ranting about being left in a room with a ghost, when there they were, dealing with a real-life tragedy. She felt horrible for Steve—just back on the job and losing his partner like that, and on his wedding night! She wondered if it was truly wise to encourage him back to work so soon. Chief Dan hadn't thought so.

She also wondered what to do about Angel. She had only met her once, the night they came for dinner and then briefly at the wedding. They weren't friends, and honestly, Penny didn't know what to think of her. She found Angel awfully quiet at the dinner, and then when they had followed her to that out-of-the-way bar, something wasn't right; something was going on. She decided she'd send her some flowers with a note to call. That way she left it up to Angel. Or maybe she'd ask Steve what to do. No, he had enough on his mind. Thinking of Steve she figured he probably wouldn't even think to eat lunch.

She snapped her laptop shut and went in the kitchen. She made a couple of sandwiches and grabbed an apple out of the bowl. She threw it all in a brown bag, grabbed her coat and headed out the door.

Steve sat quietly in the conference room and let Angel do all the talking. She had a lot to say.

It began with her telling him about the real reason she had left her job as receptionist at the law office downtown. No man was hitting on her. She knew, though, an outraged Grant would demand she quit. She was right.

The truth was she was just so tired, almost too tired to pull herself out of bed some days. When she was at work she lost all enthusiasm, and she knew her work was suffering. It could be the beginning of depression—she had many of the signs—but she couldn't admit that to herself, never mind to Grant.

She felt guilty about quitting when they needed the second income, but she couldn't help it. Then she came up with the story of starting her own business. Grant was very excited, and even she started to believe it. At first, she was so happy to not have to get up and go to work she would get up early anyway, go on the Internet, and scour for information on starting your own business. She'd print reams of information and then go over it with Grant when he got home. It was all pretty good for a while. But as the days went on she was sleeping in later and later. She soon realized she would never have the energy to start a business, let alone run one once it was started. It was all a pipe dream.

Her days became longer and longer. With nothing much else to think about, she grew obsessive over Grant. His return home from work was all she had to look forward to each day. She became terrified, wondering what she would do if anything ever happened to him. She'd scour the news reports of anything happening in the city, something in which Grant may have been involved, where he could be hurt or even killed!

That's when the anxiety started, with all the phone calls to him at work. She told Steve she would get so upset her stomach would churn and her breathing would become laboured. The only relief she could get was to hear his voice, have him reassure her he was fine.

Steve noticed Angel's hands trembling. He took both her hands and held them in his own.

"Are you OK? Do you want to continue? We could take a break."

Angel pulled her hands away and smoothed them over her hair. "No, Steve, let me finish, there's much more."

"OK, if you're sure. You know I couldn't help notice that you eventually did quit calling him at work Angel. What changed?"

"It was after you got hurt. Grant told me it wasn't my fault; it was his. He should never have taken the call. He should have been right with you when you went to talk to that kid. But I knew whose fault it really was, Steve. It was mine. I never called him at work again."

"So how did you manage the worry, the anxiety?"

"When I got worried I just forced myself to get dressed and get out of the house. I went to malls at first, a few art galleries, but it wasn't enough. One day I stopped for a coffee and noticed the VLTs. I had never gambled before and thought I'd try. I sat at that stupid machine for three hours. I couldn't believe it. It only seemed like about 20 minutes. But I won, Steve, quite a bit, and it was the greatest feeling ever."

"Let me guess, you decided to try your luck again."

"I sure did. It became like a drug to me. It was something to look forward to, something that I did on my own, and Steve, it took away the numbness. It made me feel something. Even when I lost, at least I felt something. And when I won, it was exhilarating! The only problem was, those big wins were far and few between. I was spending more and more money. Grant had no idea. He was just happy I seemed in a better mood. I knew though, how bad our finances really were."

Steve couldn't help but ask, "Where did you do all your gambling? Were you ever worried Grant would find out?"

Angel took a deep breath and began to nervously tap her fingers on the table. "Oh Steve, that's how the real trouble started, as if the rest wasn't bad enough."

Steve leaned in closer to encourage her to continue.

"I was worried Grant would find out, plus I didn't want to embarrass him by being seen out at the local bars gambling. So I drove out of town, went to an out-of-way bar. That's where I met the guy, and that's went it all went south."

Steve realized this was starting to sound like a real confession.

"There was this guy. He was always at the bar playing the VLTs at the same time I was. At first, he never spoke to me and of course, I never spoke to him either. But it was like I was invisible, like he never even noticed I was there. Often we were the only two people there. I thought this was funny, I knew I looked out of place; you'd think he'd at least be curious.

"Then one time I won a good jackpot, my machine was making all kinds of noise and the lights were blinking. He looked over at me and smiled. I couldn't help but say something. I said, finally, it's giving me some money back. He just smiled and went back to pushing the buttons on his own machine."

"Probably a good thing."

"Wait till I finish. I went home so excited. I really wanted to share the good news about my win with Grant, but how could I? But I wanted to celebrate with him somehow, so I bought a nice bottle of wine and opened it when Grant got home. He was tired, but humoured me by having one glass…one that he never finished. I had a glass before he even got home and another when he did. I really wanted to celebrate! It had been a while, you know, but I'd been so unpredictable the last while that Grant was literally scared of hurting me, upsetting me. He treated me like a china doll. When I finally convinced him I was fine, we went into the bedroom and, well, let's just say the fireworks fizzled."

Angel cast her eyes down and turned her head away from Steve.

Good thing, Steve's face was turning odd colours of red and he really wished she wasn't sharing quite so much with him. He knew though that his embarrassment was not the issue here. "It's OK. Go on."

"I blamed myself Steve, and I withdrew from Grant even more. I was no longer emotionally in our marriage. My only purpose now was the gambling. The next night I was at the bar sitting at the machine. The guy wasn't there, which I wondered at, he was always there. I was having a bad night, losing almost more than I had won the night before. Then I felt it. His warm breath on my neck, it smelled like whiskey. He whispered in my ear, called me pretty lady, asked if he could buy me a drink. I should have said no, but I wanted a drink, I wanted some company and I was almost out of money to put in the machine, I needed something."

"Please tell me you had just the one drink and left."

"I wish I could, we had a few drinks. We talked and laughed. I found out his name was Jerry, but I never told him mine. I was just called, pretty lady. Next thing I knew the bar was closing, I couldn't believe it. How could I have stayed so late? Jerry offered to walk me to my car and I let him. As soon as we were at my car he pushed me against it and started kissing me. I didn't know what to do. It was so wrong, I knew that, but I was so lonely and unhappy, Steve, and just like the VLTs it made me feel alive."

"Next thing I knew we were in the back seat. And after...well, Jerry just got up and left. He didn't say a word. He left me there in the back seat Steve, all alone. I cried my eyes out."

Steve was livid. He was angry with Jerry, but angry too with Angel. How could she be so stupid?

"Oh Steve, you must hate me now!"

"No Angel, but I do hate what you did to Grant. Is that the night you got home so late?" He softened his voice, "The night Grant hit you?"

"He told you!"

"Yeah, he felt awful, Angel."

"He shouldn't have. I deserved that and worse."

"No woman deserves that. Please, tell me you never saw this Jerry again."

"I planned not to. I really did. I was going to find a new bar to go to. But somehow, I just ended up driving back to the same bar. I wore dark glasses to hide the bruise, but when Jerry saw me he pulled them off my face. He got real mad, said no one messes up his pretty lady's face. He scared me, Steve, but I felt so worthless, I thought what does it matter what I do now. I saw him quite a few times after that. How could I do that to Grant? He was so good to me and I really did love him."

At that the tears began to flood down her face. Steve wasn't sure what to do now but when he thought of Grant he knew. He knew Grant would want him to help Angel, comfort her, no matter what she had done. He put his one arm over her shoulder and patted it gently. Angel turned to him and wrapped both her arms tightly around Steve. He felt awkward, but put his other arm around her and held her.

It was at that inopportune moment that Penny chose to walk in smiling, holding up Steve's paper bag lunch. Steve's back was to Penny, so he didn't see her mouth drop as she turned quickly and left. By time Steve pried Angel off and turned around to see who was there, Penny had left and Buddy had arrived. He was standing in the doorway holding a cup of coffee.

"Sorry Steve, didn't know you had company, just thought you could use a coffee," he said.

CHAPTER TWENTY-SIX

Well this has got to be some sort of record, Penny thought. How could he! She thought of her first husband, how he had cheated on her. At least he had waited till they had been married a few years, not a few days!

Penny realized the light had changed to green, so lost in her thoughts she hadn't even noticed. She quickly took her foot off the brake and continued driving.

She decided she was too upset to be driving yet she had no idea where to go. She couldn't go sit alone in the apartment. She considered going to see her Mom but couldn't bear to break her Mom's heart by telling her about what she saw. Steve embracing Angel, she could barely believe it herself. Then she thought of Rose. Yes, Rose, she would go see Rose.

She spent the next while concentrating on her driving and locating the turn off to where Randall and Rose lived. When she pulled in the driveway she was relieved to see the drapes open and what looked like a lot of activity inside the front window. Rose was home.

After ringing the bell she heard Rose shout from inside, "Come on in!"

Penny walked in and removed her boots in the porch. She looked for somewhere to place them, but floor space was limited. Piles of miniature boots and shoes were littered everywhere. She placed them off to the side on top of the others. There were hooks on the wall, and Penny hung her coat on the one that had the least amount of tiny parkas already hung.

"That you Penny? I'll be there in a minute. Pour yourself a coffee."

The sink was full of dishes. One bowl still had milk and some floating Cheerios. An already opened cupboard displayed a mismatch of mugs. She grabbed the closest one and as she poured her coffee she noticed it read, World's Greatest Dad.

Penny removed a laundry basket off one of the kitchen chairs and sat down. A pair of eyes peeked at her from around the hallway. Next she felt something touch her leg! She leaned over and expected to see the family dog under the table. She was surprised to instead see Daisy, their youngest daughter smiling up at her.

"Hello Daisy."

The child scooted out from under the table, giggling, and headed down the hallway.

Rose walked in the kitchen, pushing a loose strand of hair back with a wet hand. "Sorry Penny, I was just giving Randy his bath."

Penny smiled. She had almost forgotten why she had come.

Rose poured herself a cup of coffee and sat down. "Sorry about the mess." She waved her arm around the kitchen and smiled.

Penny smiled too and felt rather foolish for even coming, Rose was obviously busy.

"You OK, Penny, your eyes look a little red, dear."

"Oh no, Rose, I'm fine. You know, just worried about Steve."

"How is he doing?"

"Well he insisted on going back to work. You know he doesn't believe Grant's death was suicide."

"Steve's a smart guy, Penny."

"I know."

Penny took a long sip of her coffee and then set it down slowly. "Rose, I feel like an idiot. I went down to take him some lunch and

I walked in to find him and Angel, Grant's widow, in a very close embrace. I took one look and ran!"

"Oh Penny, I can see why that would upset you, but you shouldn't have left. I'm sure Steve could explain."

"I realize that now, but you know, I've been hurt before, but I trust Steve totally, it was just a gut reaction."

"Don't worry about it. It's nothing. Did he see you?"

"No, but Angel did, she looked right at me, never said a word. She never let go of Steve, either."

"She just lost her husband, Penny."

"I know, I know, you're right. It's just, well...I have a funny feeling about her, you know. It's awful to say, the poor thing, but just I don't trust her."

"Well intuition is nothing to be scoffed at, but you also can't presume things, you have to give people a chance, you never know what demons they face alone."

A ball rolled into the kitchen and another followed.

"Daisy!"

Penny and Rose both smiled. "I better go Rose, thanks so much, I feel so much better."

"I didn't do a thing Penny; you just needed to sort it out for yourself."

Penny reached over and gave Rose a hug. "You're a wise woman Rose, and a good friend, thanks."

When Steve walked in the door he was greeted with the welcome aroma of dinner cooking. Penny was frying pork chops, and had made mashed potatoes and a salad.

"Honey, I'm home!"

Penny laughed. "What are we, the Honeymooners?"

"Actually, yes, we are. Not your typical honeymooners but technically, we are newlyweds."

"True, but I do realize there won't be much honeymooning for a bit. How did things go today?"

"Oh pretty bad. I didn't make much headway reviewing the security tapes. I'll probably go back after dinner if you don't mind."

"No, not at all, I could come help."

"I wish you could, I could use the extra set of eyes, but I'm afraid it wouldn't be allowed."

"Anything else happen today?"

"Yeah, I had a visit from Angel, poor thing, she's a mess. I can't imagine what she's going through. I don't think she has anyone to talk to either, no family here and she's not the type to have girlfriends to talk to."

They sat down at the table to eat. Steve dug in like he'd never seen food before.

"Hungry?"

With a mouthful of food Steve just nodded.

"I went to see Rose today, what a nice home they have. I mean it's such a happy home. Randall's a lucky guy."

"Did you get any writing done?"

"No, I couldn't concentrate. What did Angel want?"

Steve filled Penny in on everything Angel had told him. All about how he thinks Angel really suffers from some kind of depression. He told her about the gambling, the debts and then Jerry, the guy she slept with. Penny tried not to react too much to the part about her cheating on Grant. It did make her think that if he had found out, it just made it even more probable that it really was a suicide.

"You still think it wasn't suicide, Steve?"

"I'm sure it wasn't."

"What about insurance? Is Angel going to be OK financially now?"

"Chief Dan looked into that. There is some kind of clause in the insurance. If the holder commits suicide in the first two years of the policy, there is no payout. Fortunately, the policy hit that two-year mark about a month ago. So even if it's deemed a suicide, which it won't be, Angel would at least get the insurance payout."

Red flags went up in Penny's head. Something is definitely not right here. Obviously if Grant knew this and they had been having financial trouble, he might do it just for Angel. And he did adore her.

Why can't Steve even entertain the idea? Or was Steve right, maybe it was purposely meant to look like suicide.

"You don't think the timing is suspicious, Steve?"

"Penny! I know what you're thinking. You're wrong." Steve put his elbows on the table, lowered his head and held it in both hands.

"It can't be suicide. If it was, then I killed him! I may as well have pulled the trigger myself."

Penny pulled her chair beside him and put her arm over his shoulders. "What are you talking about? It's not your fault in any way!"

"I knew the trouble he was in financially, his marriage was a mess and Christ, he was hitting his wife!"

"I know, Steve."

"Just once, and he felt like a bastard! Penny, it's my God damn duty to serve and protect. I couldn't even protect my own partner. I failed. The guy needed help, and I should have made sure he got it. I was trying to give him a break. If he committed suicide then it's my fault. You see now why I can't believe it."

"Oh Steve, it's not your fault, no matter what happened."

"I'm sorry Pen, I really got to go."

After Steve left, Penny sat alone at the table, heartsick. She saw the distress in his face and the way his whole body appeared to droop. It was his caring nature that made him a great detective. He worked hard and followed through. It was also what made it so difficult for him. She wanted to help him, but how could she? It was obvious that Grant's death was suicide. It just hurt Steve too much to admit it. All she could do was support him and keep her opinions to herself.

Penny settled in on the couch and wondered what more she could do to help him. Then she remembered Rose's words—Steve was a smart guy—and suddenly she had an epiphany. How could she possibly support him if she didn't believe him? He needed her to believe in him. She decided she would, and so it wasn't a suicide. Maybe, if they worked together to find a suspect, someone with motive and opportunity, they would solve a murder.

Penny sat up straight. She had a purpose, a way to help. She scoured the Internet for all the information she could find on solving a murder. She was surprised to find that often the first suspect in a murder is the spouse. Great news for a newlywed she surmised. Could Angel actually be a suspect? Penny considered what motive Angel could possibly have.

Turned out she had a lot. They had financial and marital trouble, but Angel would receive a hefty insurance payout, and with no Grant, there would be no more trouble in the marriage. No, it was a ridiculous theory. Then she remembered Grant had hit Angel. Yes, Angel definitely had motive.

Then she considered whether Angel had opportunity. Obviously she couldn't overpower Grant; he was strong, tough and trained. She did have an advantage though, he loved her deeply, trusted her. Combine that with the element of surprise and her theory had potential. Yes, this could be it, but Penny knew she had even more hope of convincing Steve that Grant had committed suicide, than the idea that Angel could have had anything to do with it. She just may have to do some investigating on her own.

First though she should consider some other options, other suspects. It could be someone Grant had arrested in the past, someone holding a grudge. She continued to search the Internet for murder cases, trying to come up with an alternative direction.

The cellphone trilled. Penny jumped. She grabbed the phone. "Hello?"

"Hi, is Steve there?"

It was a woman's voice. "No he's out, can I take a message."

"No, it's… "

"Can I tell him who called?"

"Penny? It's Angel."

"Oh, I… "

"I just needed to talk to him. Do you have his cell number?"

"Sure, what's up, everything OK?"

"Well, yes, um, no, you know, not really, I just need his help with the funeral arrangements."

"Oh, I'm so sorry." Penny gave Angel the number.

"Thanks."

The phone clicked. No goodbyes were exchanged.

Penny chided herself for her earlier suspicions, poor woman, just lost her husband. How could I possibly think she had anything to do with it? Feeling bad about it she decided to phone Steve and let him know she had called. When she did Steve thanked her for letting him know but told her he already spoke to Angel. He told Penny how he was going to pick up Angel and take her to the funeral home to make some arrangements, how Angel really had no one else to help her, and how he owed it to Grant to be there for her. Penny agreed but after hanging up she began to wonder.

Angel may just be very clever. If she did murder Grant, cozying up to Steve for help, befriending him was about the smartest thing she could do. He would never believe she had anything to do with it, no matter how incriminating the evidence was.

Penny continued to ponder this new thought.

CHAPTER TWENTY-SEVEN

Steve was getting frustrated. He had made no headway on Grant's death. As far as everyone was concerned, it was a confirmed suicide. He knew Chief Dan was only humouring him, allowing him to keep the investigation going. He wondered for how much longer. The only one who believed in him was Penny. He was grateful someone did.

The funeral had delayed his work, but he was glad he could be there for Angel. She relied on him, and he knew Grant would appreciate him being there for her. The service itself was almost unbearable, but the luncheon after was okay. Almost everyone from the force was there.

Now here he was, back in the conference room, finally making some progress on the security footage. He had taken to locking the door to minimize the interruptions and it had helped. His back was to the door when he heard a loud, authoritative knock. He pressed the stop button on the tape and turned around. When he saw it was Chief Dan he jumped up quickly and opened the door.

"What's up Chief?"

"Remind me to never doubt you again, Steve."

"You doubted me?" Steve smiled and looked at him sideways.

"Ballistics just in. You were right. It was no suicide."

Steve sat down and ran his hand through his hair.

"He was shot from at least four feet away. The gun must have been placed in his hand after the fact. We also have the approximate time of death, somewhere between two and four a.m."

"Well I've got my work cut out for me then, don't I?"

"You both do."

For the first time Steve noticed Buddy standing in the doorway.

"You're not doing this alone, Steve. Buddy here is going to work with you."

"Great." Steve sighed and pushed a chair out for Buddy with his foot. "May as well have a seat."

Chief Dan nodded at them both. He shut the door and left.

With the approximate time of death determined, they could now narrow the search on the tapes time stamps. Unfortunately, the cameras did not cover the whole area, and worse yet, did not include the crime scene, where Grant had parked his vehicle when he arrived. That would be too easy, Steve thought. The two new partners reviewed the footage from the two cameras in the parking garage. There wasn't much to watch, for there were not too many in the underground parking that time of night. A couple pulled in shortly after two. They were obviously in a hurry to get to their room. Steve and Buddy exchanged amused glances. A few staff members were seen leaving shortly after that. From then on it was pretty quiet.

Until about 2:45, when finally they had something.

"Stop it." Steve said.

One of the cameras partially recorded the double doorway into the underground parking, from the lobby. It was not very clear, but there was a figure between the doorways. They couldn't make out if it was a man or woman, although it was probably a man by the height. The face was not visible, and the figure was looking down, and wore a jacket with the hood pulled up. Steve and Buddy zoomed in, but still couldn't make out a face. When they started the tape running again they were surprised to see the person stay between the doors, pacing and every once in a while pulling at the door.

"He's locked in," Buddy said.

Steve leaned forward, closer to the screen. "Well that's strange."

Finally, a woman who looked like a staff member opened the door from the lobby. The person presumably locked between the doors pushed by her, nearly knocked her down and exited through the lobby in a hurry. The funny thing was, the staffer had no trouble opening the door from the outside, or exiting out the other.

"Hey! Isn't that the woman who found the body?" asked Buddy.

"I believe it is. Let's get her in for questioning again. She never mentioned the guy that nearly knocked her over."

"You sure it's a guy, Steve?"

"No, not sure, but I'm sure going to find out."

Steve made a copy of that part of the tape and headed home with it.

Penny had spent all afternoon on the computer. Not writing, but researching murders, trying to find some answer. Something, anything, to help Steve, she was so concerned about him. She was surprised when he walked in the door.

"You're home already."

"Already! It's six. Looks like someone got lost in their writing again."

Penny noticed Steve seemed a bit more himself, more relaxed.

"You want to order a pizza?" she asked.

"Sounds good. I have some news."

"Good news, I hope."

"No, sorry, it's not good news no matter how you look at it, but ballistics has ruled out suicide."

"Really, why?"

"Grant was shot from four feet away. He couldn't have done that himself. The gun must have been placed in his hand after."

"Oh Steve, I'm so sorry, this must be so hard for you."

"Yeah, I'm not sure which is worse. At least if it was suicide, it was his choice. This way, it's just so unfair. But it rings truer to me. I just knew Grant wouldn't have done that to himself, or to Angel."

"Any suspects?"

"As a matter of fact." Steve held up the copy of the security tape. "I really shouldn't share this with you, but I really need your opinion. Come have a look."

They sat together on the couch and watched the tape. Steve draped his arm over Penny's shoulder and she moved closer to him. It felt good. It felt like it should, not how it had been, ever since Grant's body was found. Penny felt secure, confident.

"You think the person locked between the doors is the murderer."

"Not sure Pen, very well could be. A suspect, for sure."

"Is it any help? Really, you can't see them very well. Can't even tell if it's a man or a woman."

"You're right, but the lady leaving, that's the staffer that found the body. She never mentioned the person that nearly knocked her over. We're going to question again her tomorrow."

Penny tried not to say it, but she knew she had to, no matter what his reaction.

"Steve, have you ever considered Angel as a suspect?"

"Angel, you kidding me? The poor thing is grief-stricken, doesn't know what to do with herself. No, Penny."

"It was just a thought. I know how you like to look at all angles, cover every base."

"True, but what makes you think Angel could have anything to do with this?"

Penny told him her theories, what she thought could be Angel's motives and her opportunities.

Steve had to give her credit for a compelling theory. If it weren't Angel, he might have found it half-believable.

"I know you've become very close with Angel, how you feel a duty to help her get through this Steve, and you must admit, she is a very alluring woman. Could it be clouding your view of the facts?"

"Oh come on Pen, you better not be concocting this story out of jealousy. I know your past makes you a little jittery, but you know how I feel about you. You know you can trust me."

"Oh I do. I trust you. Angel? Maybe, not so much. I brought you lunch one day. I left when I saw the two of you embracing. I never told you about it."

"Really! Is that what this is all about?"

"No, Steve! Angel saw me, you didn't. She didn't say a word, just looked at me standing foolishly in the doorway, holding your brown bag lunch. She never even let go of you, I think she may have even held you tighter when she saw me."

"That's ridiculous, she was upset. She wouldn't have done any of that intentionally."

Penny was sorry she mentioned it. She got up and went to bed.

Steve sat up for a long time. What Penny said was ludicrous. He couldn't believe her jealousy had come to this. He thought she would be much more compassionate. He watched the tape over and over again. He had to admit, assuming the person on the tape was a man might be wrong; it could be either.

He tried hard to dismiss Penny's wild theory, but the more he thought about it, the more he couldn't. Especially when he remembered the fresh tire tracks in the snow of Angel's driveway that morning he and Chief Dan went to give her the news. He'd have to check with the weather office, find out what time the fresh snow fell. See if it fit the timeline. He also better apologize to Penny.

The next morning Steve was anxious to get to work. Penny was sound asleep. He considered waking her, but decided his apology could wait. He had more pressing matters to attend to. He brushed her hair away from her forehead and gently kissed her before he left. She stirred slightly, but never woke.

CHAPTER TWENTY-EIGHT

Steve arrived at work early. Buddy was already there. He told Steve the hotel employee that had found Grant was on her way in. A couple of patrols had gone to pick her up at the hotel. He reminded Steve that her name was Barb. Steve gave Buddy a look. No one had to ever remind him of such details, but he was impressed with Buddy's work.

When Barb arrived, she looked nervous. She was wearing her hotel uniform.

"Come on in," Steve said with a smile. "Have a seat."

Her dark hair was tied back in a tight bun. Her eyes were downcast.

"Thank you," she said. She held her purse on her lap.

Steve felt sorry for her. She had suffered quite a shock from finding the body in the first place. That night when they questioned her she was visibly shaken.

"I'm missing my shift."

Buddy piped in. "You don't have to worry. I've spoken to your manager and your shift supervisor. They are well aware of the importance of you coming today. They said it's fine."

"I've already told you everything I know."

Steve looked at her. "That's true, and we thank you for that. But sometimes, when you go through such a traumatic event, as you did, some of the facts elude you, till later. We just need to follow up, and were hoping you'd look at one of the security tapes with us."

Buddy grabbed a bottle of water from the fridge and handed it to her. She looked up and smiled slightly. They reviewed her original statement and asked her if she had remembered anything else. She thought a moment, then told them no. They ran the security tape. She was surprised when she saw the person between the doors that bumped her on their way out. She could not believe she had forgotten. Steve assured her it was OK, and understandable considering the stress she was under. Unfortunately, she had nothing more to offer. She hadn't seen the person's face, and couldn't say for sure if it was a man or a woman. They asked her if she was sure there wasn't anything else she could remember, even if it seemed insignificant. She sat there awhile, quietly thinking and again shook her head and told them no, she couldn't.

Buddy said, "Well thanks for…"

"Wait! There was something, something on the person's wrist."

Buddy asked, "What—a watch? A bracelet?"

"No, it was a mark or something. I think it was red."

Steve was already rewinding the tape, looking for a shot of the person's wrist. He found one and zoomed in. There was some kind of mark on the wrist. Unfortunately when they zoomed in to see what it was, it became too distorted. Steve and Buddy were excited now. She said it was red; it could be blood.

"Buddy, call IT, tell them to come get this tape right away, see if they can sharpen the image, make out what this is. It could be the break we need. And tell them today!"

Buddy made the call and Steve started asking Barb about the locked doors that trapped the person between them.

"They weren't locked. I walked in one and out the other. I ought to know, and you could see that yourself. Plus, they are never locked; guests have to be able to get to their cars."

Steve scratched his head. "I realize that, but you watched the tape before you got there. The person couldn't get out; they tried both doors several times."

Barb gripped the handles of her purse a little more tightly. "Well, there is one other explanation."

Buddy was done his call and was now listening intently. They both leaned in closer to hear what she had to say.

"I'm not sure I should say anything."

Steve leaned back in his chair, crossed his arms and took a deep breath. "You know Barb, this is very important, a man is dead. Whatever you have to say could be very helpful."

"OK, but you'll think I'm crazy."

"I can assure you we won't, now please, go ahead."

"Alright. Well you must have heard before that the hotel is haunted."

Buddy stood and threw his arms in the air in exasperation.

Barb looked sideways at him, but Steve was nodding, urging her to continue.

"Most people have only heard about Room 202, the one where the young bride-to-be hung herself in the closet. Poor thing. I never go in that room, never have, never will. If tending to that room is on my shift, everyone knows, someone else has to do it. I sense things a little stronger than some, you know. Once I was…"

"I'm sorry Barb, we are in the middle of an investigation here, as much as we'd love to hear your ghost stories, I think we're done here."

"No!" Steve barked. "Let her finish."

Buddy made a quizzical face, but sat down anyway.

"The dining room has many ghosts. We hear them—terrible sounds—but when someone goes to investigate the noise, there's no one there! And many of us have heard unexplained crying and talking throughout the hotel, but it's the lobby where I sense a very strong presence. It doesn't scare me as much as the others."

She paused and looked up at Steve. "I don't know why, but it's almost a comfort, like it's watching over things, perhaps, a former employee. One who has passed and maybe still on the job?"

"So how would these ghosts have anything to do with the doors locking shut?"

"You have to admit, there's no reasonable explanation they'd be locked one minute and not the next. If the person was up to no good, maybe the lobby ghost saw something, thought locking them between the doors might help?"

Steve got up. "You know Barb, about a year ago I might have dismissed such things. Don't get me wrong, I certainly don't believe in ghosts. I just…well, I don't disbelieve as strongly as I used to. And I certainly don't think you're crazy."

Barb smiled at Steve, sneered at Buddy, and got up from her chair. He held her one elbow and guided her to the door.

"Thank you so much for coming in. You've really been very helpful."

Steve shut the door and heard a loud bang. Buddy was beside himself with laughter and was slamming his hand on the table.

Steve couldn't help but smile himself, but he still tried to get Buddy to quiet down, in case Barb could hear him as she was leaving. At least his new partner had a sense of humour.

While Buddy composed himself from his laughing fit, Steve's mood shifted. He sat with a worried look on his face. He was hoping Barb would confirm the person was a male. If so, it would rule out Angel's involvement. Unfortunately it hadn't.

"Buddy, I have a theory, one I'm not too happy about. We better get Chief Dan in on this."

Steve sat in the room alone, running the events of the evening through his head. He just couldn't believe how things were looking. Maybe Penny was right. Maybe Angel was snowing him, playing the grieving widow, befriending him to avert any suspicion from her. He had hoped a pretty face couldn't dupe him so easily.

When Chief Dan and Buddy returned, Steve told them both everything he knew. How Angel had a bad gambling addiction that was causing them a lot of financial grief. He told them how Angel was suffering from depression, how she had cheated on Grant. With a lump in his throat he told them about the day Grant admitted to hitting Angel. Steve tried to explain that part as best he could. He wanted them to understand how bad Grant felt, that it was a one-time thing and would never have happened again.

Then he told them his theory. Angel went home, changed into dark clothes, a jacket with a hood. She grabbed Grant's gun and drove back to the hotel. That's when she sent him the text to come home. She knew he would. She waited in the parking garage for him to get in his car. She didn't have to worry about overpowering him; he wasn't afraid of her, and she had the element of surprise. Then she simply walked up to the car, opened the passenger door and shot him. After, she placed his gun in his hand and put up her hood and ran to make a quick exit. The only problem was she got locked between the doors. She was lucky though, Barb showed up just in time to allow her getaway. The red mark on the wrist was likely her husband's blood.

Chief Dan frowned. "You've been holding back a lot of information, Steve."

"I know, I'm sorry, I was just trying to be a good friend to Grant. And the stuff about Angel, I really never considered her a suspect in my wildest dreams, so none of it seemed relevant."

"What was her motive?" Buddy asked. "I mean, some is obvious, she was seeing someone else, but if she wanted to be with the new guy, couldn't she have just got a divorce?"

"I think it was for money, the insurance policy. And maybe the fact that Grant hit her had put a worse taste in her mouth than she admitted."

Chief Dan added, "And it was timely, the suicide clause for non-payment of suicide in the first two years of the policy was coincidently just over."

"She has no alibi either," Steve added. "She claims she was home alone with a headache, no one to substantiate that. Plus, there were tire tracks in the driveway the morning Dan and I went to give her the news."

"She sure played the part of a grieving wife perfectly," said Chief Dan, shaking his head. "We better bring her in."

CHAPTER TWENTY-NINE

Steve was deluding himself. Penny knew he was an extremely competent detective with a great record, but this time it was all just too close. Grant was his partner, his friend, and they had grown close very quickly. Then there was Steve's guilt. When he became aware of Grant's troubles he was in one of those damned if you do, damned if you don't situations. Of course, with the way things had turned out, Steve was dealing with a heavy load of guilt.

Then there was Angel, poor, helpless and drop-dead gorgeous Angel. Steve felt an obligation to her because of Grant, Penny understood that, but she was pretty sure Angel was no angel. She had a lot to gain from Grant's death and if Steve couldn't see it, she sure could.

After last night, she knew he wouldn't listen to any more of her accusations against Angel. It was futile. No, she would have to find some concrete evidence herself, before she could broach the subject again. And she knew just where to start.

But first a transformation had to take place. Penny dug into her still-packed suitcase from the wedding. It still sat on the floor in the bedroom. She grabbed the case that held the hot rollers and plugged them in on the bathroom sink. She hated these rollers; for the life of her, she couldn't figure how one was supposed to put them in without burning their fingers. She ran to the front closet and grabbed her leather gloves to protect her fingers from the heat. As she rolled up her hair she smiled, amused, at her reflection. She was wearing her baggy grey sweatsuit and leather gloves, and her head was now full of rollers.

While her hair set she dug in her suitcase again to find her wedding shoes—white pumps, perfect. She pulled her tightest, darkest jeans out of the bureau drawer, and after removing her sweatsuit, she put on the jeans, then slipped the pumps on her feet. The green sweater Steve had bought her for Christmas hung in the closet. Realizing she'd never stretch it over the rollers, she decided it was time for them to come out. She was pleased to see the wavy curls that fell on her shoulders. She grabbed the silly push-up bra, the one she had bought at a weak moment, out of the drawer, and pulled on her green sweater. Back in the bathroom she barely recognized the woman in the mirror as she layered on black eyeliner and mascara. She finished with a rich coral lipstick. The effect was exactly what she wanted. She grabbed her white trench coat, the one she never wore, out of the front closet and dashed out the door.

Her plan was still percolating in her mind. She had a hunch that the bar where Steve and she had followed Angel might hold some answers. Someone might know something that would help her, especially if she happened to run into Angel's new boyfriend. She knew too that she wouldn't get too far with him if she went in her regular garb. If he had been attracted to Angel, she had to emulate her, somewhat, to get his attention. She was anxious to get there and drove fast, just edging over the limit.

When she pulled in the parking lot she was excited, but as she got out of her car and headed to the entrance she quickly lost her nerve. She wondered if this was such a good idea after all. No, I'm here, she thought, I can do this, I have to, for Steve.

As she walked through the first door, the smell hit her hard—stale beer and cigarette smoke. The stench got worse as she pushed through the second door. It was just past noon, and the place was almost empty. Her eyes had trouble adjusting to the dimness. An older man sat at the end of the bar, nursing a beer and staring at the TV that hung over the bar. A basketball game was playing out on the screen, but there was no sound from the TV. Instead, some canned music thumped in the background. Penny walked towards the bar and sat on a stool. The older man, just two stools away, never took his eyes off the game. Penny smiled brightly at the tired server behind the counter.

"Do you have any water in a bottle?"

The server had long black hair and was wearing faded jeans and a tight black tank top that sported the name of the bar across her chest. Without looking up from her magazine she replied, "No."

Penny was getting nervous and worried. How was she ever going to get any information? She had to do something.

"How about a Jack Daniels, straight up, no ice." She had heard her Dad order this before.

This time the server did look up.

"You sure."

"Why not."

The server poured her the shot and placed it in front of her. The glass looked a little cloudy and Penny thought she could detect some old lipstick on the rim.

"You going to drink it, or stare at it?" The man watching basketball had taken notice.

"Well, sure I am." She looked at the server, "And, please, bring this gentleman one too, I'm buying."

The server poured another and slid it down the bar. Then she leaned both elbows on the bar and rested her face on her palms, and stared at Penny.

Penny lifted her glass and said, "Down the hatch!" She took one sip and started to choke.

The man and the server both laughed.

"How about I get you a glass of Coke?"

Penny tried to clear her throat and animatedly nodded yes!

Deciding she'd never get anywhere with these two now, Penny headed over to the VLTs. She was relieved Steve had shown her how to play. She set her Coke down and selected a machine in the middle. No one else was playing. She inserted a 10-dollar bill and began to press buttons. She only bet one credit at a time, in hopes of stretching out her time without adding more money. Amazingly she was winning. Her 10 was now over 40 dollars. She was almost forgetting why she was there, until she felt it. A warm breath on her neck, then a whisper.

"Well hello, pretty lady, I knew you'd come back."

"How could I stay away?" Penny whispered back. But as soon as she spoke he knew it wasn't her.

"Sorry, thought you were someone else."

He walked over to a machine at the end and sat down to play.

Now what? Now what? Penny pressed Collect Winnings, grabbed her ticket and moved down to a machine a bit closer.

"Not having much luck over there," she announced to make an excuse for her move. He said nothing.

They both played silently for the longest time. It was driving her crazy. She knew she looked damn good; why wasn't he bothering with her? She finally had to say something.

"How you doing, any luck?"

"Is there something you want?" He looked up at her. "Pretty lady."

Penny blushed. "No, well, maybe just some company." She couldn't believe she said that!

"Let's go have a drink then." He got up, and motioned with his arm for her to go first. As he walked past the bar he held up two fingers to the server. He pulled out a chair for her and then sat himself down in the one right beside her. The server set a beer down in front of him and another Coke in front of Penny. Penny thought she banged his beer down on the table a little harder than necessary. Some of the foam started rising and he quickly grabbed it and stuck the neck of the bottle in his mouth, his eyes never leaving hers.

"So you think I'm a pretty lady?"

"Damn straight you are."

"I bet you see a lot of pretty ladies come through here."

He smiled, "Not usually, but lately, it's like angels are falling from the sky."

"Angels?" Penny was excited. This had to be the guy!

He was starting to look a little angry. "You ask a lot of questions, pretty lady."

She knew she better not arouse any more suspicion, for a bit anyway. She tilted her head and smiled at him.

"Only when I'm with such interesting company."

"Well that you are." He took a long slow sip of his beer. "What brings you here today pretty lady?"

This was a good opening. "I left my husband, and I'm tired of sitting around the house."

"Really now, what kind of fool husband would let you out of his grip?"

"A real bastard. He started knocking me around. I wasn't staying for that."

He looked at her suspiciously again and got up. "I gotta take a piss."

Penny noticed the guy at the bar was no longer watching basketball and the server wasn't flipping through her magazine; both were looking her way. She smiled sheepishly knowing she had likely failed, the guy was probably gone. She went and paid her bill and headed to the door.

"Hey, pretty lady, leaving so soon."

Penny jumped, it was like he came out of nowhere and was right beside her.

"Yeah, I have to go. Maybe we'll see you again. What was your name?"

"It's Jerry, and, guess what? I'm on my way out too. I'll walk to your car. It's not the best neighbourhood."

Penny wanted to turn back, go back in where it was safe, then figured she was just being silly.

"Sure, thanks."

He whistled with his hands in his pocket as he followed her to her car.

"I'm fine, really. You don't have to walk me to my car."

"Don't mind at all, pretty lady."

She was sorry for where she had parked now. She hadn't wanted her car to be seen and had parked in the rear of the lot by a group of trees.

"Thank you. Bye."

Before she knew what was happening he had her pinned against her car with his body. He had grabbed both her wrists and held her arms above her head. She squirmed but he was too big, too strong. He put his other hand around her throat and lifted her chin up with his thumb. He glared at her.

"Why all the questions?"

She could barely speak; her throat was tight.

"No…reason."

He laughed. "You remind me of another pretty lady." At that he leaned his face into hers and let go of her throat. Instead he grabbed a clump of her hair and pulled her head back. She could smell the beer on his breath and cigarette smoke; she felt like throwing up. He pressed his body against her even harder, and then he forced the worst kiss of her life on her. Tears ran down her face and her mind screamed out for Steve.

Steve was a wreck. He sat alone in the coffee room. He had called Angel and told her she needed to come in and answer a few questions. He had been cold and distant on the phone, official. He had told her a couple of officers would pick her up, and when she said it wasn't necessary, she could drive herself, he was firm, no, they'd pick her up. He knew she was waiting in the interrogation room. He knew now that she had used him, but worst of all she had killed Grant. He literally felt sick to the stomach.

Delaying the inevitable, he decided to call Penny. He had overreacted to her accusations against Angel. Imagine, accusing her of being jealous. He could be such a jerk! Turns out she was right all along. He wanted to apologize, but more than anything, he wanted to hear her voice. He knew that would help. Disappointed after a few tries with no answer, he gave up.

Buddy stuck his head in the coffee room. "You ready, she's here."

Steve got up slowly, "Yeah, sure, may as well get this over with."

Chief Dan was already in place sitting outside the two-way window of the interrogation room. He held a folder, and a pencil sat behind his ear.

"You ready for this Steve?"

They all looked at Angel. She sat fidgeting, looking around the room at the bare grey walls.

Steve just nodded as he and Buddy opened the door and went in.

"Steve!" Angel jumped up. "What's going on? They wouldn't even let me change."

Angel wore a sweatsuit; it was nothing like Penny's. Angel's pants were black and very snug fitting. A somewhat plunging white v-neck T-shirt fit nicely under her pink hooded sweater. Her hair was held up in a scattered mess with one large clip.

Steve turned away. "You do it, Buddy."

"Angel Mayne, you are under arrest for the murder of your husband, Grant Mayne…"

"What the hell? Steve! Grant wasn't murdered! He committed suicide. You said so!"

Angel slumped into her chair. She looked so confused, so helpless. Steve really wanted to comfort her. He thought of Grant, how much he had loved her. He managed to hold his ground.

"I'm sorry Angel, ballistics came in, there's no way he could have shot himself from four feet away."

Angel began to cry. "Well how could you think I could do this, I was at home, I loved him Steve, you know that!"

"I know you wanted me to believe that, and truly, I think I wanted to believe you, but the evidence proves otherwise."

The interrogation went on for a long time. Buddy was writing down her statement. Angel was wearing down, and just as they suspected, her story began to change.

"Okay, yes, I lied about that night. I never took a taxi home from the hotel. I never had a headache. I just had to get out of there. I was so miserable. Steve, you and Penny, you were so happy you were goddamn glowing. I couldn't bear it. I took the taxi to a bar, I went to gamble."

"Gamble, or meet your friend?" Steve asked.

"Just gamble. I never wanted to see that guy again, and if I did, I was going to tell him just that!"

"And did you see him, what was his name, Jerry?"

"Yeah, I did."

"Then what happened?"

"He offered me a ride home when the bar closed. I would have said no, but my taxi was taking forever and it was cold outside."

Buddy felt the urge to finally ask one of the questions, "Did you have sexual relations with him that evening."

"No! What does that have to do with it?"

"Never mind, just tell us what did happen," Steve said.

"Well, we drove around for awhile then he stopped in my driveway. I told him I couldn't ever see him again, I needed, wanted, to make things right with my husband."

"How did he take that?"

"At first he didn't believe me, couldn't believe I'd want to be with a guy who doesn't appreciate me, a guy who hits me. I explained that it was out of character, that he would never do it again. He got mad, grabbed my face and said something like no one hits my angel face!"

"Did he hurt you?"

"No, not really. When I told him I loved my husband with all my heart, that being with him those nights was a big mistake, a huge lapse in judgment and that I regretted it horribly, he told me to get out."

"Did you?"

"Yes. That was the end of it. I went in the house and went to bed. I decided to tell Grant everything the next day. See if he still wanted me; tell him I needed some help."

"The next day? Then why did you send him the text?"

"What text?"

"The one you used to lure him into the parking lot, Angel, don't toy with me now."

"I don't know what you're talking about Steve. I don't know anything about a text!"

Steve was confused; he wasn't sure what direction to go in now. "We're going to need you to give us your cellphone now for evidence."

"I wish I could. I lost it that night, the night Grant died."

She began with the tears again. Buddy looked at Steve and rolled his eyes. Steve got up.

"Excuse us a moment." He gestured for Buddy to follow.

Once outside Steve said, "We need to find her cellphone."

"What for? We have Grant's. The record of her text is on his phone."

"I just like to be thorough."

Chief Dan got up. "That's fine; I'll send a couple patrols to her home to look around the yard and the street. I'll also send some to the Hotel Fort Garry. See if we can't find it for you, Steve."

"There's somewhere we need to go, Buddy. Dan, can you make sure she's taken care of, get her a sandwich or something."

"Sure, Steve, you go ahead, I'll check with IT too, see how they're doing with the tape."

CHAPTER THIRTY

"Where we off to?"

Steve was weaving through traffic at a fast pace. He had placed the cherry light on the side of the roof.

"I got a hunch, there's someone we need to talk to."

"Who?"

"That Jerry guy, we need him to collaborate Angel's story."

"Well it's true then, you really are a stickler for details, but why the hurry, Angels not going anywhere—for a long time I might add."

"I just don't want to waste a lot of time. I want to check the bar where they meet, see if he's there."

"Well I hate to be a stickler for details, but I really don't think we need to be in that big of a rush and endanger our city pedestrians."

Steve slowed down. He rolled down the window and pulled the cherry back in the car. Buddy shut the light off.

"I just feel it's important that we get there quick."

They reached the turnoff for the highway and Steve accelerated again.

"It's just up here a bit."

As they pulled in the parking lot, Buddy pointed to the back edge of the lot.

"Look! You were right to get here in a hurry. Looks like that lady could use some help."

Steve saw a large man holding the throat of a young woman. He had her pinned against the car with his body. As Steve pulled in they saw the guy yank her head back by her hair. He was forcing himself on her. She was squirming to get away and Steve thought he heard a muffled scream.

Steve and Buddy both jumped out of the car and went running over to where they were. The slamming of their doors alarmed the man and he turned around. It was then that the man fell to his knees, screaming.

That was when he saw her! Penny?

Steve grabbed the man off the ground and threw him against the car. He wanted to smash his face into the pavement, but he knew better. Instead he twisted the man's arms behind his back and started putting the cuffs on him.

The man twisted his head around and sneered maliciously at Steve, "Hey, whatta ya doin'? Me and my pretty lady were just having some fun. You know how it is, she likes it a little rough."

Steve recognized the face but couldn't immediately place it.

"You're under arrest."

"For what?"

"Assault."

"You kidding me, I told you we were just having some fun, if anyone assaulted anyone, it was her! She kneed me right in the cojones—fuckin' hard, too!

"That is one tough pretty lady, she also happens to be my wife!"

"Ah fuck, can't you pigs keep your fuckin' women at home anymore?"

It was then that Steve realized where he had seen this scum before. He was the guy from the house, the one he and Grant went to his first day back, the day he was stabbed. They had brought him in later for questioning. He was the one that got away, the one with the solid alibi.

Steve looked over at Penny; she was shaking. Buddy had draped his own coat over her shoulders and was holding her close for support.

"Hey, Buddy! Throw this piece of shit in the back seat for me."

"Love to, Steve."

While Buddy complied with his request, Steve hurried over to Penny. "You OK?"

"Yeah, I'm not hurt, I'll be OK, but Steve, I was so scared. How did you know to come?"

"I didn't, or maybe I did. I don't know. I'm just glad I did."

"I'm so sorry, I was trying to…"

"I'm dying to know what the hell you were doing here Pen, why the hell you look like this, but it's going to have to wait. I'll get Buddy to drive your car back to the station. You're going to have to come make a statement so we can hold this guy."

The drive back to the station was quiet. Penny was beyond embarrassed. At first, Buddy tried to engage her in conversation. He told her his name really was Buddy, he knew how Steve calls everybody Buddy if he couldn't remember, or didn't know their name. Penny smiled and nodded in agreement. She didn't feel much like talking. She felt horrible and wondered what Steve must be thinking. When Buddy told her he was Steve's new partner she became a little more interested. She was glad; he seemed like a pretty nice guy. He was young and very tall and muscular. Penny figured he had blond hair, though it was tough to be sure when it was totally shaved off. She couldn't understand why all these young guys wanted to go around with no hair. She loved Steve's thick hair.

"I'm glad you're his partner. Steve could sure use a friend right now."

Buddy smiled and nodded knowingly in agreement. Penny leaned her head against the window and gazed out at the road. It was hard to keep quiet when she had a million questions. Mainly, she wanted to find out why they drove out to the bar. She also wanted to explain what she was doing there herself. She couldn't imagine what Buddy must be thinking. She decided though, for once, she'd keep her mouth shut, to avoid making any more of a mess for Steve at work than she already had. They drove the rest of the way in silence.

When they arrived at the station, Jerry was already in an interrogation room. Angel still waited in the other. She was tired and very nervous. Chief Dan had kept his promise and got her a sandwich, even a few magazines. She hadn't touched either.

Steve and Chief Dan were conferring in the room outside the windows of both rooms.

Penny and Buddy walked in. The first thing Penny noticed was Angel, pacing in the room on the other side of the glass. Chief Dan's back was to them and Steve was too preoccupied to notice them come in. Dan said, "Well Steve, good work. Now that you've officially charged her with the murder, you better give her a chance to call a lawyer, even if she doesn't want one, and do it before you ask her any more questions."

Penny couldn't believe what she was hearing! Steve had charged Angel with Grant's murder! She wondered what changed his mind. He was so sure last night that she had nothing to do with it. She looked at Angel. The woman really did look pitiful, and Penny could see why Steve had a hard time believing Angel capable of murder, but thank God he did.

"Will do, Chief and this joker." Steve pointed to the room where Jerry was sitting, leaning back in his chair looking morose. "I want to talk to him myself, because he roughed up Penny pretty good. He's going to get what he deserves."

Penny couldn't keep quiet any longer, "Steve, I'm pretty sure he's the guy Angel was hooking up with!"

Steve was surprised to see Penny in the room. Buddy shrugged his shoulders apologetically. Penny shouldn't be privy to the conversations going on, even if she was Steve's wife.

"No kidding! You sure, Pen?"

"Well no, but he said something to me about angels falling from the sky, I just thought…"

"It's a stretch, but you just might be onto something. If it is, he's just the guy I want to talk to."

"You better get her out of here," Chief Dan said.

"I'll take her down to give a statement," Buddy offered.

"Steve, I…"

"Later, Pen. Sorry, this is important. And hurry back, Buddy. Get one of the other officers to take her statement."

Steve looked at Chief Dan. "Before we get Angel all lawyered up, I need to talk to this guy, find out if he really is Angel's boyfriend. If he is, I'll need him to corroborate what Angel said, plus a few things still aren't adding up. I think he might be just the guy to clear it up for me."

When Buddy got back they both went in the room to question Jerry. The man was confused with the line of questioning. He asked how they knew so much about him and Angel. He was getting agitated. He thought he was just here to be charged for assault of the lady in the parking lot.

"We just need you to fill us in on a few facts about the evening of February 14th."

"Why?"

"Well, that's the evening my partner, your Angel's husband, was murdered in the parking garage of the Hotel Fort Garry."

"Murdered? Angel told me he committed suicide, shot himself or something."

At first he tried to say he never saw Angel that night at all. Tried to say he was with some other lady all evening, he could call the lady, she'd tell them. Steve wasn't putting up with any bullshit. He told Jerry there were tire tracks in Angel's driveway, showed him the picture he took of the tire tracks on his phone, and then suggested if they checked them against the tires on his car there would be a match. Steve told him that a tire tread was as individual as a fingerprint. He wasn't sure if this was true, but it was enough to get him to admit that he was with Angel that night.

The guy was a snake. He lied through his teeth as much as he could get away with, which wasn't much with Steve. Buddy was impressed, but couldn't figure out what Steve hoped to get out it. They already knew what happened. Angel was already arrested.

There was a heavy knock at the door.

Buddy opened the door to see Chief Dan. "I need to talk to you boys a minute."

"Hey, can I get something to drink, I'm damn near parched."

Steve glared at Jerry. "Yeah, sure, as soon as hell freezes over." He turned. "What *is it*, Dan?"

"Hold that tone for someone else, Steve. They found her phone. Someone turned it in to the hotel reception desk at the hotel. They had found it out back in the lane."

"Did you send it for prints?"

"I did Steve, and I put a rush on it for you."

"Good, we better get back in there."

"One more thing." Dan handed an envelope to Steve. "IT managed to get a pretty detailed picture from the tape. I think you better look at it right away."

Steve already had it out of the envelope and was staring at it. "Holy shit!" He thrust the envelope and picture into Buddy's hands and rushed back into the interrogations room. Buddy ran after him before he could even look at the picture. Steve grabbed Jerry's arm and pushed his sleeve up. And there it was, on his wrist, a tattoo of a red spider with a skull face. Buddy looked at the picture; it was the same as the tattoo.

That was it, Steve wound up like he was going to punch the guy into next week. Thankfully, Buddy saw it coming and grabbed Steve's fist and stopped him—just in time. Chief Dan was in the room now too. "Take it easy Steve."

"What the hell is going on here, this is fucking brutality! I'm not saying another word until I get a lawyer."

Steve left the room and went straight to Angel. Buddy had the pleasure of informing Jerry that he was under arrest for the murder of Detective Grant Mayne, and proceeded to read him his Miranda rights.

"Steve! What's going on? I've been here forever. You can't really believe I murdered Grant!"

"No I can't Angel, I never really did; it just all pointed that way for a while. I'm real sorry."

Steve put his arm around her shoulder, "Come on, let's get you out of here."

Penny had finished her statement long ago and had been sitting in the coffee room sipping on a horrible cup of coffee. She forced herself to drink it, knowing she needed some caffeine and likely deserved worse for her day's antics. Despite it all, she was relieved Steve had finally seen through Angel's deception. Not knowing whether she should leave or not, she had stayed for quite some time. She finally decided she couldn't wait anymore. She left the coffee room and headed down the hallway to find Steve, or someone, to tell her what was going on, what she should do. And there they were, Steve and Angel walking towards her—Steve holding her close. Angel's eyes were red and swollen; fresh tears were falling down her cheeks.

"Steve?"

"Penny, come with us."

Steve led them all into the conference room and shut the door. He explained to them how he had made a big mistake arresting Angel. He should have known better, should have trusted his instincts. Penny fidgeted uncomfortably in her chair. He broke the news that Jerry was being held for Grant's murder. Both women gasped for their own reasons.

"No, Steve, I killed him," Angel admitted quietly. "If I had never met Jerry, none of this would have happened."

"No, Angel, you can't think that way. You're not responsible for that scum and what he did."

"What am I going to do now?" Angel wailed. "I have no one."

"That's not true Angel, you have Steve—and me."

Steve looked at Penny with admiration.

"Yes you do and we're going to get you some help. I'm going to call a friend of mine; he's a good guy. He's helped me get over a few hurdles. Penny, can you stay with Angel, I'm going to call Phil Cleaver, get him to come see her."

"Sure." Penny pulled her chair close to Angel and put her own arm around her shoulders. "We'll be fine. You go do what you have to do."

"Thanks, Pen."

CHAPTER THIRTY-ONE

Chief Dan had insisted this time, that Steve take a whole week off. He did.

Penny and Steve sat on the couch at the apartment. It was really the first time they had to talk since the arrest.

Penny tilted her head and looked at Steve, "So you mean Angel never really sent the text to Grant?"

"Nope. When she told Jerry she wanted nothing more to do with him, he kicked her out of the car. She left so fast she didn't realize she had dropped her phone in his car."

"And that's when Jerry saw the opportunity, came up with a plan, right?"

"Yeah, the poor sap thought if Angel wanted to patch things up with Grant, the only chance he had with her was if Grant wasn't in the picture. The guy had never met a lady like Angel. He had it bad for her."

"I bet in his own twisted way he even rationalized that he was doing her a favour."

Steve was confused by her logic, "Why do you say that?"

"Well, he knew Grant had hit her, from his lifestyle he might have just expected it to get a lot worse."

"Maybe. I doubt it. He doesn't seem like the kind of guy that would worry too much about it. You see how he treated you."

Penny remembered the humiliation and snuggled closer to Steve. "Yeah, I see your point."

Steve wrapped his one arm around her. "More likely he was banking on her getting a big insurance payout. That could solve both their money problems. The guy wasn't smart enough to know about the suicide clause, just got lucky on that one."

"So how did you get a conviction?"

"It's always in the evidence, Pen. He had motive and opportunity, but to get a conviction, you have to rely on the evidence to remove any doubt. His prints were on Angel's phone, proving it was him who sent the text, then there was the tire treads that matched his car, proving he had been to Angel's. Mainly, it was his red spider tattoo, the one on his wrist. It was a perfect match for the one on the person trapped between the doors of the parking garage. That placed him at the scene of the crime, smack in the middle of the time of death window."

"But Steve, how did Jerry get Grant's gun?"

"I only have a theory for now. For some reason Grant must have brought his gun to our wedding, I don't know why. But he must have had it with him, or in the car. Somehow Jerry got a hold of it. He likely sent the text and then either broke into Grant's car and waited, hiding in the backseat and then surprised him, or he was lurking in the shadows. We're still working on that."

Penny rested her head on Steve's shoulder. "How did he ever get himself locked between the doors?"

"That I don't know, not sure if we ever will, but I know a lady who works at the hotel who has some thoughts. You might want to meet her."

"Why would I want to meet her?"

"She claims it was the ghost from the lobby who helped trap the suspect."

"Really?"

"Yeah, but before I tell you anymore, I need you to tell me what the hell you were doing, dressed the way you were, in that parking lot with a murderer!"

"Oh shit. I guess I do have some explaining."

After a late night of talking everything out, both of them went to bed and almost fell asleep before their heads hit the pillow. Over breakfast the next day Steve announced that they owed each other a proper wedding night. Penny was wearing her baggy grey sweatsuit and stood at the stove scrambling some eggs. She had just had a shower and her hair fell straight and still wet. Steve thought she looked stunning as she turned and smiled, "I guess we do."

Steve was surprised when she wanted to go back to Room 202 at the Hotel Fort Garry, back where it had all started. When he asked her why, she had said it just felt right. It would be like a replay, another chance to a proper start to their marriage. Besides, she really wanted to actually spend the whole night in the haunted room, but made him promise not to leave her alone!

Steve had laughed and made the promise again.

"Let's go tonight," she said.

Steve called, and as luck would have it, the room was available.

Penny's suitcase still lay on the bedroom floor. Inside was pretty much everything she needed, including her wedding night outfit. She put it on the bed, removed a few things and then closed the cover and zipped it up.

"I'm ready to go."

"What, already!"

Steve threw a few things in a bag and they headed out. They promised this evening was just about them, there would be no talk of recent tragedies. They checked in and went to the Palm Room at the hotel for dinner. It was a fabulous room to dine and they proceeded to go through the formalities of dinner. They chatted about mundane things, the weather, or the lack of spring weather, and how much snow there was that year. Penny talked about her family, her Dad. She told Steve that before he retired he had been an industrial salesman and that he and the salesmen would often frequent the Palm Room themselves, for lunch. She laughed when she told them how he'd regale stories of them competing to see who could steal the most butter patties. Apparently there used to be an extra charge. Steve laughed at her stories and told a few of his own.

When the waitress asked if they were ready for dessert, they both smiled, and said yes, and left. They went straight to their room. It was already getting dark and Penny switched on the end table lamp. While Steve was in the bathroom she quickly slipped on her white lace garter and the matching bra. She sat at the vanity and rolled on her nylons and fastened them to the garter. When Steve walked out of the bathroom he stopped and stared. She hadn't heard him come out and he stood silently while he watched her carefully roll on the last nylon. He walked over, took her hand and she stood up. He held her at a distance and admired her.

"You are absolutely beautiful. What on earth are you doing with an ape like me?"

"Oh you'll do for now," she teased.

He led her to the bed and they slipped between the sheets. He kissed her gently and then—nothing. Absolutely nothing!

Penny looked at the clock on the bedside table. An hour had passed. She looked down; she had nothing on! What the hell happened? She couldn't remember a thing. Did she fall asleep? Did she black out? She couldn't let Steve know. He was looking at her, smiling dreamily. Not knowing what else to do or say, she put her arm over his chest and snuggled close. "That was wonderful, wasn't it?"

"It sure was." He leaned over and kissed her forehead. His mind was reeling. He too looked at the clock and realized a full hour had passed. Why couldn't he remember anything? He couldn't have fallen asleep; it was as if he had been drugged, or had a memory lapse of some sort. Great, he thought, finally he gets his wedding night with Penny and he missed it. The room was dark, but the bathroom light was still on, the door slightly ajar. It cast a stream of light over Penny's body. Dare he?

"Would I be such a beast to suggest another go at it?"

Penny laughed, relieved, "May as well, the room is paid for."

He leaned over her.

"Steve!"

"Hmmm?"

"Look," she pointed to the door. It was wide open to the hallway.

"Steve, shut the door!"

EPILOGUE

"Come Nadine, we can go now."

"Oh William, I do love you so. It was the most wonderful evening of my life."

"As it was mine"

The two of them floated down the hallway, Nadine in her wedding dress with her beautiful cloak draped over her shoulders.

"You were gone so long, William."

"Now I told you Nadine, a man has to make a living."

They floated down the stairwell, into the lobby and directly out the front door.

"You best put your hood up dear, there seems to be a fresh snowfall."